THE COLLECTED WORKS OF ALDOUS HUXLEY

★

LIMBO

By ALDOUS HUXLEY

Novels

CROME YELLOW
ANTIC HAY
THOSE BARREN LEAVES
POINT COUNTER POINT
BRAVE NEW WORLD
BRAVE NEW WORLD REVISITED
EYELESS IN GAZA
AFTER MANY A SUMMER
TIME MUST HAVE A STOP
APE AND ESSENCE
THE GENIUS AND THE GODDESS
ISLAND

Short Stories

LIMBO
MORTAL COILS
LITTLE MEXICAN
TWO OR THREE GRACES
BRIEF CANDLES
COLLECTED SHORT STORIES

Biography

GREY EMINENCE
THE DEVILS OF LOUDUN

Essays and Belles Lettres

ON THE MARGIN
ALONG THE ROAD
PROPER STUDIES
DO WHAT YOU WILL
MUSIC AT NIGHT &
VULGARITY IN LITERATURE
TEXTS AND PRETEXTS (Anthology)
THE OLIVE TREE
ENDS AND MEANS (An Enquiry
into the Nature of Ideals)
THE ART OF SEEING
THEMES AND VARIATIONS
THE PERENNIAL PHILOSOPHY
SCIENCE, LIBERTY AND PEACE
THE DOORS OF PERCEPTION
HEAVEN AND HELL
ADONIS AND THE ALPHABET
COLLECTED ESSAYS
LITERATURE AND SCIENCE

Travel

JESTING PILATE
BEYOND THE MEXIQUE BAY
BEYOND THE MEXIQUE BAY (Illustrated)

Poetry and Drama

VERSES AND A COMEDY
(including early poems, Leda, The Cicadas
and The World of Light, a Comedy)
THE GIOCONDA SMILE

For Children

THE CROWS OF PEARBLOSSOM

LETTERS OF ALDOUS HUXLEY

LIMBO

Six Stories and A Play

By

ALDOUS HUXLEY

1970

CHATTO & WINDUS

LONDON

PUBLISHED BY

Chatto & Windus

LONDON

✳

Clarke, Irwin & Co. Ltd.
TORONTO

ISBN 0 7011 0805 3

First published 1920
First issued in a Collected Edition 1946
Reprinted 1950 and 1962
First issued in this edition 1970

Applications regarding translation rights in any
work by Aldous Huxley should be addressed to
Chatto & Windus, 40 William IV Street, London,
W.C.2

Printed in Great Britain by
Lewis Reprints Limited,
Port Talbot, Glamorgan

CONTENTS

LIMBO

FARCICAL HISTORY OF RICHARD GREENOW

I

THE most sumptuous present that Millicent received on her seventh birthday was a doll's house. " With love to darling little Mill from Aunty Loo." Aunt Loo was immensely rich, and the doll's house was almost as grandiose and massive as herself.

It was divided into four rooms, each papered in a different colour and each furnished as was fitting : beds and wash-stands and wardrobes in the upstair rooms, arm-chairs and artificial plants below. " Replete with every modern convenience ; sumptuous appointments." There was even a cold collation ready spread on the dining-room table—two scarlet lobsters on a dish, and a ham that

1

had been sliced into just enough to reveal
an internal complexion of the loveliest
pink and white. One might go on talking about the doll's house for ever, it was
so beautiful. Such, at any rate, was the
opinion of Millicent's brother Dick. He
would spend hours opening and shutting
the front door, peeping through the
windows, arranging and rearranging the
furniture. As for Millicent, the gorgeous
present left her cold. She had been
hoping—and, what is more, praying,
fervently, every night for a month—that
Aunty Loo would give her a toy sewing-
machine (one of the kind that works,
though) for her birthday.

She was bitterly disappointed when the
doll's house came instead. But she bore
it all stoically and managed to be wonderfully polite to Aunty Loo about the whole
affair. She never looked at the doll's
house : it simply didn't interest her.

Dick had already been at a preparatory
school for a couple of terms. Mr. Killigrew, the headmaster, thought him a
promising boy. " Has quite a remarkable
aptitude for mathematics," he wrote in
his report. " He has started Algebra

this term, and shows a "—"quite remarkable " scratched out (the language of reports is apt to be somewhat limited)— " a very unusual grasp of the subject." Mr. Killigrew didn't know that his pupil also took an interest in dolls : if he had, he would have gibed at Dick as unmercifully and in nearly the same terms as Dick's fellow-schoolboys—for shepherds grow to resemble their sheep and pedagogues their childish charges. But of course Dick would never have dreamt of telling anyone at school about it. He was chary of letting even the people at home divine his weakness, and when anyone came into the room where the doll's house was, he would put his hands in his pockets and stroll out, whistling the tune of, " There is a Happy Land far, far away, where they have Ham and Eggs seven times a day," as though he had merely stepped in to have a look at the beastly thing—just to give it a kick.

When he wasn't playing with the doll's house, Dick spent his holiday time in reading, largely, devouringly. No length or incomprehensibility could put him off ; he had swallowed down *Robert Elsmere* in

the three-volume edition at the age of
eight. When he wasn't reading he used
to sit and think about Things in General
and Nothing in Particular ; in fact, as
Millicent reproachfully put it, he just
mooned about. Millicent, on the other
hand, was always busily doing something :
weeding in the garden, or hoeing, or
fruit-picking (she could be trusted not to
eat more than the recognized tariff—one
in twenty raspberries or one in forty
plums) ; helping Kate in the kitchen ;
knitting mufflers for those beings known
vaguely as The Cripples, while her mother
read aloud in the evenings before bed-
time. She disapproved of Dick's mooning,
but Dick mooned all the same.

When Dick was twelve and a half he
knew enough about mathematics and
history and the dead languages to realize
that his dear parents were profoundly
ignorant and uncultured. But, what was
more pleasing to the dear parents, he
knew enough to win a scholarship at
Æsop College, which is one of our
Greatest Public Schools.

If this were a Public School story, I
should record the fact that, while at

Æsop, Dick swore, lied, blasphemed, repeated dirty stories, read the articles in *John Bull* about brothels disguised as nursing-homes and satyrs disguised as curates; that he regarded his masters, with very few exceptions, as fools, not even always well-meaning. And so on. All which would be quite true, but beside the point. For this is not one of the conventional studies of those clever young men who discover Atheism and Art at School, Socialism at the University, and, passing through the inevitable stage of Sex and Syphilis after taking their B.A., turn into maturely brilliant novelists at the age of twenty-five. I prefer, therefore, to pass over the minor incidents of a difficult pubescence, touching only on those points which seem to throw a light on the future career of our hero.

It is possible for those who desire it—incredible as the thing may appear—to learn something at Æsop College. Dick even learnt a great deal. From the beginning he was the young Benjamin of his mathematical tutor, Mr. Skewbauld, a man of great abilities in his own art, and who, though wholly incapable of keeping a form in order, could make his private tuition a source of much profit to a mathematically minded boy. Mr. Skewbauld's house was the worst in Æsop : Dick described it as a mixture between a ghetto and a home for the mentally deficient, and when he read in Sir Thomas Browne that it was a Vulgar Error to suppose that Jews stink, he wrote a letter to the *School Magazine* exploding that famous doctor as a quack and a charlatan, whose statements ran counter to the manifest facts of everyday life in Mr. Skewbauld's house. It may seem surprising that Dick should have read Sir Thomas Browne at all. But he was more than a mere mathematician. He filled the ample leisure, which is Æsop's most precious gift to those of its Alumni who know how to use it, with much and varied reading in history, in literature, in physical science, and in more than one foreign language. Dick was something of a prodigy.

" Greenow's an intellectual," was Mr. Copthorne-Slazenger's contemptuous verdict. " I have the misfortune to have two or three intellectuals in my house.

They're all of them friends of his. I think he's a Bad Influence in the School." Copthorne-Slazenger regarded himself as the perfect example of *mens sana in corpore sano*, the soul of an English gentleman in the body of a Greek god. Unfortunately his legs were rather too short and his lower lip was underhung like a salmon's.

Dick had, indeed, collected about him a band of kindred spirits. There was Partington, who specialized in history ; Gay, who had read all the classical writings of the golden age and was engaged in the study of mediæval Latin ; Fletton, who was fantastically clever and had brought the art of being idle to a pitch never previously reached in the annals of Æsop. These were his chief friends, and a queer-looking group they made—Dick, small and dark and nervous ; Partington, all roundness, and whose spectacles were two moons in a moonface ; Gay, with the stiff walk of a little old man ; and Fletton, who looked like nobody so much as Mr. Jingle, tall and thin with a twisted, comical face.

" An ugly skulking crew," Copthorne-

Slazenger, conscious of his own Olympian splendour, would say as he saw them pass.

With these faithful friends Dick should have been — and indeed for the most part was—very happy. Between them they mustered up a great stock of know- ledge ; they could discuss every subject under the sun. They were a liberal education and an amusement to one another. There were times, however, when Dick was filled with a vague, but acute, discontent. He wanted something which his friends could not give him ; but what, but what ? The discontent rankled under the surface, like a sup- pressed measles. It was Lord Francis Quarles who brought it out and made the symptoms manifest.

Francis Quarles was a superb creature, with the curly forehead of a bull and the face and limbs of a Græco-Roman statue. It was a sight worth seeing when he looked down through half-shut eyelids, in his usual attitude of sleepy arrogance, on the world about him. He was in effect what Mr. Copthorne-Slazenger imagined himself to be, and he shared that gentleman's dislike for Dick and his friends. "Yellow little atheists," he called them. He always stood up for God and the Church of England ; they were essential adjuncts to the aristocracy. God, indeed, was almost a member of the Family ; lack of belief in Him amounted to a personal insult to the name of Quarles.

It was half-way through the summer term, when Dick was sixteen, on one of those days of brilliant sunshine and cloudless blue, when the sight of beautiful and ancient buildings is peculiarly poignant. Their age and quiet stand out in melancholy contrast against the radiant life of the summer ; and at Æsop the boys go laughing under their antique shadow ; "Little victims"—you feel how right Gray was. Dick was idly strolling across the quadrangle, engaged in merely observing the beauty about him — the golden-grey chapel, with its deep geometrical shadows between the buttresses, the comely rose-coloured shapes of the brick-built Tudor buildings, the weathercocks glittering in the sun, the wheeling flurries of pigeons. His old discontent had seized on him again, and to-day in

2

the presence of all this beauty it had
become almost unbearable. All at once,
out of the mouth of one of the dark little
tunnelled doors pierced in the flanks of
the sleeping building, a figure emerged
into the light. It was Francis Quarles,
clad in white flannels and the radiance
of the sunshine. He appeared like a
revelation, bright, beautiful, and sudden,
before Dick's eyes. A violent emotion
seized him ; his heart leapt, his bowels
were moved within him ; he felt a
little sick and faint—he had fallen in
love.

Francis passed by without deigning
to notice him. His head was high, his
eyes drowsy under their drooping lids.
He was gone, and for Dick all the light
was out, the beloved quadrangle was a
prison-yard, the pigeons a loathsome flock
of carrion eaters. Gay and Partington
came up behind him with shouts of
invitation. Dick walked rudely away.
God ! how he hated them and their
wretched, silly talk and their yellow, ugly
faces.

The weeks that followed were full
of strangeness. For the first time in his

life Dick took to writing poetry. There was one sonnet which began :

Is it a vision or a waking dream?
Or is it truly Apollo that I see,
Come from his sylvan haunts in Arcady
To {laugh and loiter
    {sing and saunter by an English stream. . .

He kept on repeating the words to himself, " Sylvan haunts in Arcady," " laugh and loiter " (after much thought he had adopted that as more liquidly melodious than " sing and saunter "). How beautiful they sounded !—as beautiful as Keats—more beautiful, for they were his own.

He avoided the company of Gay and Fletton and Partington ; they had become odious to him, and their conversation, when he could bring himself to listen to it, was, somehow, almost incomprehensible. He would sit for hours alone in his study ; not working—for he could not understand the mathematical problems on which he had been engaged before the fateful day in the quadrangle—but reading novels and the poetry of Mrs. Browning, and at intervals writing something rather ecstatic of his own. After a long preparatory screwing up of his courage, he dared at last to send a fag with a note to Francis, asking him to tea ; and when Francis rather frigidly refused, he actually burst into tears. He had not cried like that since he was a child.

He became suddenly very religious. He would spend an hour on his knees every night, praying, praying with frenzy. He mortified the flesh with fasting and watching. He even went so far as to flagellate himself—or at least tried to ; for it is very difficult to flagellate yourself adequately with a cane in a room so small that any violent gesture imperils the bric-à-brac. He would pass half the night stark naked, in absurd postures, trying to hurt himself. And then, after the dolorously pleasant process of self-maceration was over, he used to lean out of the window and listen to the murmurs of the night and fill his spirit with the warm velvet darkness of midsummer. Copthorne-Slazenger, coming back by the late train from town one night, happened to see his moon-pale face hanging out of window and was delighted to be able to give him two hundred Greek lines to remind him that even a member of the Sixth Form requires sleep sometimes.

The fit lasted three weeks. " I can't think what's the matter with you, Greenow," complained Mr. Skewbauld snufflingly. " You seem incapable or unwilling to do anything at all. I suspect the cause is constipation. If only everyone would take a little paraffin every night before going to bed! . . ." Mr. Skewbauld's self-imposed mission in life was the propagation of the paraffin habit. It was the universal panacea—the cure for every ill.

His friends of before the crisis shook their heads and could only suppose him mad. And then the fit ended as suddenly as it had begun.

It happened at a dinner-party given by the Cravisters. Dr. Cravister was the Headmaster of Æsop—a good, gentle, learned old man, with snow-white hair and a saintly face which the spirit of comic irony had embellished with a nose that might, so red and bulbous it was, have been borrowed from the properties of a music-hall funny man. And then there was Mrs. Cravister, large and stately as a galleon with all sails set. Those who met her for the first time might be awed by the dignity of what an Elizabethan would have called her " swelling port." But those who knew her well went in terror of the fantastic spirit which lurked behind the outward majesty. They were afraid of what that richly modulated voice of hers might utter. It was not merely that she was malicious—and she had a gift of ever-ready irony ; no, what was alarming in all her conversation was the element of the unexpected. With most people one feels comfortably secure that they will always say the obvious and ordinary things ; with Mrs. Cravister, never. The best one could do was to be on guard and to try and look, when she made a more than usually characteristic remark, less of a bewildered fool than one felt.

Mrs. Cravister received her guests— they were all of them boys — with stately courtesy. They found it pleasant to be taken so seriously, to be treated as perfectly grown men ; but at the same time, they always had with Mrs. Cravister a faint uncomfortable suspicion that all her politeness was an irony so exquisite as to be practically undistinguishable from ingenuousness.

" Good evening, Mr. Gay," she said, holding out her hand and shutting her eyes ; it was one of her disconcerting habits, this shutting of the eyes. " What a pleasure it will be to hear you talking to us again about eschatology."

Gay, who had never talked about eschatology and did not know the meaning of the word, smiled a little dimly and made a protesting noise.

" Eschatology ?   What a charming subject ! "   The fluty voice belonged to Henry Cravister, the Headmaster's son, a man of about forty who worked in the British Museum.   He was almost too cultured, too erudite.

" But I don't know anything about it," said Gay desperately.

" Spare us your modesty," Henry Cravister protested.

His mother shook hands with the other guests, putting some at their ease with a

charming phrase and embarrassing others
by saying something baffling and unexpected that would have dismayed even the
hardiest diner-out, much more a schoolboy tremblingly on his good behaviour.
At the tail end of the group of boys stood
Dick and Francis Quarles. Mrs. Cravister
slowly raised her heavy waxen eyelids and
regarded them a moment in silence.

"The Græco-Roman and the Gothic
side by side!" she exclaimed. "Lord
Francis is something in the Vatican, a
rather late piece of work; and Mr.
Greenow is a little gargoyle from the
roof of Notre Dame de Paris. Two
epochs of art—how clearly one sees the
difference. And my husband, I always
think, is purely Malayan in design—
purely Malayan," she repeated as she
shook hands with the two boys.

Dick blushed to the roots of his hair,
but Francis' impassive arrogance remained unmoved. Dick stole a glance
in his direction, and at the sight of his
calm face he felt a new wave of adoring
admiration sweeping through him.

The company was assembled and complete. Mrs. Cravister looked round the

room and remarking, "We won't wait for Mr. Copthorne-Slazenger," sailed majestically in the direction of the door. She particularly disliked this member of her husband's staff, and lost no opportunity of being rude to him. Thus, where an ordinary hostess might have said, "Shall we come in to dinner?" Mrs. Cravister employed the formula, "We won't wait for Mr. Copthorne-Slazenger"; and a guest unacquainted with Mrs. Cravister's habits would be surprised on entering the dining-room to find that all the seats at the table were filled, and that the meal proceeded smoothly without a single further reference to the missing Copthorne, who never turned up at all, for the good reason that he had never been invited.

Dinner began a little nervously and uncomfortably. At one end of the table the Headmaster was telling anecdotes of Æsop in the sixties, at which the boys in his neighbourhood laughed with a violent nervous insincerity. Henry Cravister, still talking about eschatology, was quoting from Sidonius Apollinarius and Commodianus of Gaza. Mrs.

Cravister, who had been engaged in a long colloquy with the butler, suddenly turned on Dick with the remark, " And so you have a deep, passionate fondness for cats," as though they had been intimately discussing the subject for the last hour. Dick had enough presence of mind to say that, yes, he did like cats— all except those Manx ones that had no tails.

" No tails," Mrs. Cravister repeated— " no tails. Like men. How symbolical everything is ! "

Francis Quarles was sitting opposite him, so that Dick had ample opportunity to look at his idol. How perfectly he did everything, down to eating his soup ! The first lines of a new poem began to buzz in Dick's head :

"All, all I lay at thy proud marble feet—
 My heart, my love and all my future days.
 Upon thy brow for ever let me gaze,
 For ever touch thy hair : oh (something) sweet . . ."

Would he be able to find enough rhymes to make it into a sonnet ? Mrs. Cravister, who had been leaning back in her chair for the last few minutes in a state of exhausted abstraction, opened her eyes and said to nobody in particular :

" Ah, how I envy the calm of those Chinese dynasties ! "

" Which Chinese dynasties ? " a well-meaning youth inquired.

" Any Chinese dynasty, the more remote the better. Henry, tell us the names of some Chinese dynasties."

In obedience to his mother, Henry delivered a brief disquisition on the history of politics, art, and letters in the Far East.

The Headmaster continued his reminiscences.

An angel of silence passed. The boys, whose shyness had begun to wear off, became suddenly and painfully conscious of hearing themselves eating. Mrs. Cravister saved the situation.

" Lord Francis knows all about birds," she said in her most thrilling voice. " Perhaps he can tell us why it is the unhappy fate of the carrion crow to mate for life."

Conversation again became general. Dick was still thinking about his sonnet. Oh, these rhymes !—praise, bays, roundelays, amaze : greet, bleat, defeat, beat, paraclete. . . .

> " . . . to sing the praise
> In anthems high and solemn roundelays
> Of Holy Father, Son and Paraclete."

That was good—damned good ; but it hardly seemed to fit in with the first quatrain. It would do for one of his religious poems, though. He had written a lot of sacred verse lately.

Then suddenly, cutting across his ecstatic thoughts, came the sound of Henry Cravister's reedy voice.

"But I always find Pater's style so *coarse*," it said.

Something explosive took place in Dick's head. It often happens when one blows one's nose that some passage in the labyrinth connecting ears and nose and throat is momentarily blocked, and one becomes deaf and strangely dizzy. Then, suddenly, the mucous bubble bursts, sound rushes back to the brain, the head feels clear and stable once more. It was something like this, but transposed into terms of the spirit, that seemed now to have happened to Dick.

It was as though some mysterious obstruction in his brain, which had dammed up and diverted his faculties from their normal course during the past three weeks, had been on a sudden overthrown. His life seemed to be flowing once more along familiar channels.

He was himself again.

"But I always find Pater's style so *coarse*."

These few words of solemn foolery were the spell which had somehow performed the miracle. It was just the sort of remark he might have made three weeks ago, before the crisis. For a moment, indeed, he almost thought it was he himself who had spoken ; his own authentic voice, carried across the separating gulf of days, had woken him again to life !

He looked at Francis Quarles. Why, the fellow was nothing but a great prize ox, a monstrous animal. "There was a Lady loved a Swine. Honey, said she . . ." It was ignoble, it was ridiculous. He could have hidden his face in his hands for pure shame ; shame tingled through his body. Goodness, how grotesquely he had behaved !

He leaned across and began talking to Henry Cravister about Pater and style and books in general. Cravister was amazed at the maturity of the boy's mind; for he possessed to a remarkable degree that critical faculty which in the vast majority of boys is—and from their lack of experience must be—wholly lacking.

"You must come and see me some time when you're in London," Henry Cravister said to him when the time came for the boys to get back to their houses. Dick was flattered; he had not said that to any of the others. He walked home with Gay, laughing and talking quite in his old fashion. Gay marvelled at the change in his companion; strange, inexplicable fellow! but it was pleasant to have him back again, to repossess the lost friend. Arrived in his room, Dick sat down to attack the last set of mathematical problems that had been set him. Three hours ago they had appeared utterly incomprehensible; now he understood them perfectly. His mind was like a giant refreshed, delighting in its strength.

Next day Mr. Skewbauld congratulated him on his answers.

"You seem quite to have recovered your old form, Greenow," he said. "Did you take my advice? Paraffin regularly . . ."

Looking back on the events of the last weeks, Dick was disquieted. Mr. Skewbauld might be wrong in recommending paraffin, but he was surely right in supposing that something was the matter and required a remedy. What could it be? He felt so well; but that, of course, proved nothing. He began doing Müller's exercises, and he bought a jar of malt extract and a bottle of hypophosphites. After much consultation of medical handbooks and the encyclopædia, he came to the conclusion that he was suffering from anæmia of the brain; and for some time one fixed idea haunted him: Suppose the blood completely ceased to flow to his brain, suppose he were to fall down suddenly dead or, worse, become utterly and hopelessly paralysed. . . . Happily the distractions of Æsop in the summer term were sufficiently numerous and delightful to

divert his mind from this gloomy brooding, and he felt so well and in such high
spirits that it was impossible to go on
seriously believing that he was at death's
door. Still, whenever he thought of
the events of those strange weeks he was
troubled. He did not like being con-
fronted by problems which he could
not solve. During the rest of his stay
at school he was troubled by no more
than the merest velleities of a relapse.
A fit of moon-gazing and incapacity to
understand the higher mathematics had
threatened him one time when he was
working rather too strenuously for a
scholarship. But a couple of days'
complete rest had staved off the peril.
There had been rather a painful scene,
too, at Dick's last School Concert. Oh,
those Æsop concerts ! Musically speaking, of course, they are deplorable ; but
how rich from all other points of view
than the merely æsthetic ! The supreme
moment arrives at the very end when
three of the most eminent and popular
of those about to leave mount the platform together and sing the famous
" Æsop, Farewell." Greatest of school

songs! The words are not much, but the tune, which goes swooning along in three-four time, is perhaps the master-piece of the late organist, Dr. Pilch.

Dick was leaving, but he was not a sufficiently heroic figure to have been asked to sing, " Æsop, Farewell." He was simply a member of the audience, and one, moreover, who had come to the concert in a critical and mocking spirit. For, as he had an ear for music, it was impossible for him to take the concert very seriously. The choir had clamor-ously re-crucified the Messiah; the soloists had all done their worst; and now it was time for " Æsop, Farewell." The heroes climbed on to the stage. They were three demi-gods, but Francis Quarles was the most splendid of the group as he stood there with head thrown back, eyes almost closed, calm and appar-ently unconscious of the crowd that seethed, actually and metaphorically, beneath him. He was wearing an enormous pink orchid in the buttonhole of his evening coat; his shirt-front twinkled with diamond studs; the buttons of his waistcoat were of fine

3

gold. At the sight of him, Dick felt his heart beating violently ; he was not, he painfully realized, master of himself.

The music struck up—Dum, dum, dumdidi, dumdidi ; dum, dum, dum, and so on. So like the *Merry Widow*. In two days' time he would have left Æsop for ever. The prospect had never affected him very intensely. He had enjoyed himself at school, but he had never, like so many Æsopians, fallen in love with the place. It remained for him an institution ; for others it was almost an adored person. But to-night his spirit, rocked on a treacly ocean of dominant sevenths, succumbed utterly to the sweet sorrow of parting. And there on the platform stood Francis. Oh, how radiantly beautiful ! And when he began, in his rich tenor, the first verse of the Valedictory :

> "Farewell, Mother Æsop,
>   Our childhood's home !
> Our spirit is with thee,
>   Though far we roam . . ."

he found himself hysterically sobbing.

II

CANTELOUP COLLEGE is per-
haps the most frightful building
in Oxford—and to those who know their
Oxford well this will mean not a little.
Up till the middle of last century Canteloup possessed two quadrangles of fifteenth-
century buildings, unimpressive and petty,
like so much of College architecture, but
at least quiet, unassuming, decent. After
the accession of Victoria the College
began to grow in numbers, wealth, and
pride. The old buildings were too small
and unpretentious for what had now
become a Great College. In the summer
of 1867 a great madness fell upon the
Master and Fellows. They hired a most
distinguished architect, bred up in the
school of Ruskin, who incontinently
razed all the existing buildings to the
ground and erected in their stead a vast
pile in the approved Mauro-Venetian
Gothic of the period. The New Buildings contained a great number of rooms,
each served by a separate and almost
perpendicular staircase ; and if nearly

half of them were so dark as to make it necessary to light them artificially for all but three hours out of the twenty-four, this slight defect was wholly outweighed by the striking beauty, from outside, of the Neo-Byzantine loopholes by which they were, euphemistically, " lighted."

Prospects in Canteloup may not please ; but man, on the other hand, tends to be less vile there than in many other places. There is an equal profusion at Canteloup of Firsts and Blues ; there are Union orators of every shade of opinion and young men so languidly well bred as to take no interest in politics of any kind ; there are drinkers of cocoa and drinkers of champagne. Canteloup is a microcosm, a whole world in miniature ; and whatever your temperament and habits may be, whether you wish to drink, or row, or work, or hunt, Canteloup will provide you with congenial companions and a spiritual home.

Lack of athletic distinction had prevented Dick from being, at Æsop, a hero or anything like one. At Canteloup, in a less barbarically ordered state of society, things were different. His rooms in the

Venetian gazebo over the North Gate became the meeting-place of all that was most intellectually distinguished in Canteloup and the University at large. He had had his sitting-room austerely upholstered and papered in grey. A large white Chinese figure of the best period stood pedestalled in one corner, and on the walls there hung a few uncompromisingly good drawings and lithographs by modern artists. Fletton, who had accompanied Dick from Æsop to Canteloup, called it the " cerebral chamber " ; and with its prevailing tone of brain-coloured grey and the rather dry intellectual taste of its decorations it deserved the name.

To-night the cerebral chamber had been crammed. The Canteloup branch of the Fabian Society, under Dick's presidency, had been holding a meeting. " Art in the Socialist State " was what they had been discussing. And now the meeting had broken up, leaving nothing but three empty jugs that had once contained mulled claret and a general air of untidiness to testify to its having taken place at all. Dick stood leaning an elbow on the mantelpiece and absent-mindedly kicking, to the great detriment of his pumps, at the expiring red embers in the grate. From the depths of a huge and cavernous arm-chair, Fletton, pipe in mouth, fumed like a sleepy volcano.

"I liked the way, Dick," he said, with a laugh—"the way you went for the Arty-Crafties. You utterly destroyed them."

"I merely pointed out, what is sufficiently obvious, that crafts are not art, nor anything like it, that's all." Dick snapped out the words. He was nervous and excited, and his body felt as though it were full of compressed springs ready to jump at the most imponderable touch. He was always like that after making a speech.

"You did it very effectively," said Fletton. There was a silence between the two young men.

A noise like the throaty yelling of savages in rut came wafting up from the quadrangle on which the windows of the cerebral chamber opened. Dick started; all the springs within him had gone off at once—a thousand simultaneous Jack-in-the-boxes.

"It's only Francis Quarles' dinner-party becoming vocal," Fletton explained. " Blind mouths, as Milton would call them."

Dick began restlessly pacing up and down the room. When Fletton spoke to him, he did not reply or, at best, gave utterance to a monosyllable or a grunt.

" My dear Dick," said the other at last, "you're not very good company to-night," and heaving himself up from the arm-chair, Fletton went shuffling in his loose, heelless slippers towards the door. " I'm going to bed."

Dick paused in his lion-like prowling to listen to the receding sound of feet on the stairs. All was silent now : Gott sei dank. He went into his bedroom. It was there that he kept his piano, for it was a piece of furniture too smugly black and polished to have a place in the cerebral chamber. He had been thirsting after his piano all the time Fletton was sitting there, damn him ! He drew up a chair and began to play over and over a certain series of chords. With his left hand he struck an octave G in the base, while his right dwelt lovingly on F, B, and E. A luscious chord, beloved by Mendelssohn—a chord in which the native richness of the dominant seventh is made more rich, more piercing sweet by the addition of a divine discord. G, F, B, and E—he let the notes hang tremulously on the silence, savoured to the full their angelic overtones ; then, when the sound of the chord had almost died away, he let it droop reluctantly through D to the simple, triumphal beauty of C natural— the diapason closing full in what was for Dick a wholly ineffable emotion.

He repeated that dying fall again and again, perhaps twenty times. Then, when he was satiated with its deliciousness, he rose from the piano and opening the lowest drawer of the wardrobe pulled out from under his evening clothes a large portfolio. He undid the strings ; it was full of photogravure reproductions from various Old Masters. There was an almost complete set of Greuze's works, several of the most striking Ary Scheffers, some Alma Tadema, some Leighton, photographs of sculpture by Torwaldsen and Canova, Boecklin's " Island of the Dead," religious pieces by Holman Hunt, and a large packet of miscellaneous pictures from the Paris Salons of the last forty years.

He took them into the cerebral chamber where the light was better, and began to study them, lovingly, one by one. The Cézanne lithograph, the three admirable etchings by Van Gogh, the little Picasso looked on, unmoved, from the walls.

It was three o'clock before Dick got to bed. He was stiff and cold, but full of the satisfaction of having accomplished something. And, indeed, he had cause to be satisfied; for he had written the first four thousand words of a novel, a chapter and a half of *Heartsease Fitzroy : the Story of a Young Girl.*

Next morning Dick looked at what he had written overnight, and was alarmed. He had never produced anything quite like this since the days of the Quarles incident at Æsop. A relapse? He wondered. Not a serious one in any case; for this morning he felt himself in full possession of all his ordinary faculties. He must have got overtired speaking to the Fabians in the evening. He looked at his manuscript again, and read : "'Daddy, do the little girl angels in heaven have toys and kittens and teddy-bears ?'

"'I don't know,' said Sir Christopher

gently. 'Why does my little one
ask ? '

" ' Because, daddy,' said the child—
' because I think that soon I too may be
a little angel, and I should so like to
have my teddy-bear with me in heaven.'

" Sir Christopher clasped her to his
breast. How frail she was, how ethereal,
how nearly an angel already ! Would
she have her teddy-bear in heaven ?
The childish question rang in his ears.
Great, strong man though he was, he was
weeping. His tears fell in a rain upon
her auburn curls.

" ' Tell me, daddy,' she insisted, ' will
dearest God allow me my teddy-bear ? '

" ' My   child,'   he   sobbed,   ' my
child . . .' "

The blushes mounted hot to his cheeks ;
he turned away his head in horror. He
would really have to look after himself
for a bit, go to bed early, take exercise,
not do much work. This sort of thing
couldn't be allowed to go on.

He went to bed at half-past nine that
night, and woke up the following morning to find that he had added a dozen or
more closely written pages to his original

manuscript during the night. He supposed he must have written them in
his sleep. It was all very disquieting.
The days passed by; every morning a
fresh instalment was added to the rapidly
growing bulk of *Heartsease Fitzroy*. It
was as though some goblin, some Lob-lie-
by-the-Fire, came each night to perform
the appointed task, vanishing before
the morning. In a little while Dick's
alarm wore off; during the day he was
perfectly well; his mind functioned
with marvellous efficiency. It really
didn't seem to matter what he did in his
sleep provided he was all right in his
waking hours. He almost forgot about
Heartsease, and was only reminded of
her existence when by chance he opened
the drawer in which the steadily growing
pile of manuscript reposed.

In five weeks *Heartsease Fitzroy* was
finished. Dick made a parcel of the
manuscript and sent it to a literary agent.
He had no hopes of any publisher taking
the thing; but he was in sore straits for
money at the moment, and it seemed
worth trying, on the off-chance. A
fortnight later Dick received a letter

beginning : " DEAR MADAM,—Permit me to hail in you a new authoress of real talent. *Heartsease Fitzroy* is GREAT,"— and signed " EBOR W. SIMS, Editor, *Hildebrand's Home Weekly*."

Details of the circulation of *Hildebrand's Home Weekly* were printed at the head of the paper ; its average net sale was said to exceed three and a quarter millions. The terms offered by Mr. Sims seemed to Dick positively fabulous. And there would be the royalties on the thing in book form after the serial had run its course.

The letter arrived at breakfast ; Dick cancelled all engagements for the day and set out immediately for a long and solitary walk. It was necessary to be alone, to think. He made his way along the Seven Bridges Road, up Cumnor Hill, through the village, and down the footpath to Bablock Hithe, thence to pursue the course of the " stripling Thames "—haunted at every step by the Scholar Gipsy, damn him ! He drank beer and ate some bread and cheese in a little inn by a bridge, farther up the river ; and it was there, in the inn

parlour, surrounded by engravings of the
late Queen, and breathing the slightly
mouldy preserved air bottled some three
centuries ago into that hermetically sealed
chamber—it was there that he solved
the problem, perceived the strange truth
about himself.

He was a hermaphrodite.

A hermaphrodite, not in the gross
obvious sense, of course, but spiritually.
Two persons in one, male and female.
Dr. Jekyll and Mr. Hyde : or rather a
new William Sharp and Fiona MacLeod
—a more intelligent William, a vulgarer
Fiona. Everything was explained ; the
deplorable Quarles incident was simple
and obvious now. A sentimental young
lady of literary tastes writing sonnets to
her Ouida guardsman. And what an
unerring flair Mr. Sims had shown by
addressing him so roundly and unhesi-
tatingly as " madam " !

Dick was elated at this discovery. He
had an orderly mind that disliked
mysteries. He had been a puzzle to
himself for a long time ; now he was
solved. He was not in the least distressed
to discover this abnormality in his char-

acter. As long as the two parts of him kept well apart, as long as his male self could understand mathematics, and as long as his lady novelist's self kept up her regular habit of writing at night and retiring from business during the day, the arrangement would be admirable. The more he thought about it, the more it seemed an ideal state of affairs. His life would arrange itself so easily and well. He would devote the day to the disinterested pursuit of knowledge, to philosophy and mathematics, with perhaps an occasional excursion into politics. After midnight he would write novels with a feminine pen, earning the money that would make his unproductive male labours possible. A kind of spiritual *souteneur*. But the fear of poverty need haunt him no more ; no need to become a wage-slave, to sacrifice his intelligence to the needs of his belly. Like a gentleman of the East, he would sit still and smoke his philosophic pipe while the womenfolk did the dirty work. Could anything be more satisfactory ?

He paid for his bread and beer, and walked home, whistling as he went.

III

TWO months later the first instalment of *Heartsease Fitzroy: the Story of a Young Girl*, by Pearl Bellairs, appeared in the pages of *Hildebrand's Home Weekly*. Three and a quarter millions read and approved. When the story appeared in book form, two hundred thousand copies were sold in six weeks; and in the course of the next two years no less than sixteen thousand female infants in London alone were christened Heartsease. With her fourth novel and her two hundred and fiftieth Sunday paper article, Pearl Bellairs was well on her way to becoming a household word.

Meanwhile Dick was in receipt of an income far beyond the wildest dreams of his avarice. He was able to realize the two great ambitions of his life—to wear silk underclothing and to smoke good (but really good) cigars.

I V

DICK went down from Canteloup in a blaze of glory. The most brilliant man of his generation, exceptional mind, prospects, career. But his head was not turned. When people congratulated him on his academic successes, he thanked them politely and then invited them to come and see his Memento Mori. His Memento Mori was called Mr. Glottenham and could be found at any hour of the day in the premises of the Union, or if it was evening, in the Senior Common Room at Canteloup. He was an old member of the College, and the dons in pity for his age and loneliness had made him, some years before, a member of their Common Room. This act of charity was as bitterly regretted as any generous impulse in the history of the world. Mr. Glottenham made the life of the Canteloup fellows a burden to them ; he dined in Hall with fiendish regularity, never missing a night, and he was always the last to leave the Common Room. Mr. Glottenham did not prepossess at a first glance ;

the furrows of his face were covered with a short grey sordid stubble ; his clothes were disgusting with the spilth of many years of dirty feeding ; he had the shoulders and long hanging arms of an ape—an ape with a horribly human look about it. When he spoke, it was like the sound of a man breaking coke ; he spoke incessantly and on every subject. His knowledge was enormous ; but he possessed the secret of a strange inverted alchemy — he knew how to turn the richest gold to lead, could make the most interesting topic so intolerably tedious that it was impossible, when he talked, not to loathe it.

This was the death's-head to which Dick, like an ancient philosopher at a banquet, would direct the attention of his heartiest congratulators. Mr. Glottenham had had the most dazzling academic career of his generation. His tutors had prophesied for him a future far more brilliant than that of any of his contemporaries. They were now Ministers of State, poets, philosophers, judges, millionaires. Mr. Glottenham frequented the Union and the Canteloup

4

Senior Common Room, and was—well,
he was just Mr. Glottenham. Which
was why Dick did not think too highly
of his own laurels.

V

"WHAT shall I do? What ought I
to do?" Dick walked up and
down the room smoking, furiously and
without at all savouring its richness, one
of his opulent cigars.

"My dear," said Cravister—for it was
in Cravister's high-ceilinged Bloomsbury
room that Dick was thus unveiling his
distress of spirit—"my dear, this isn't a
revival meeting. You speak as though
there were an urgent need for your soul
to be saved from hell fire. It's not as bad
as that, you know."

"But it *is* a revival meeting," Dick
shouted in exasperation—"it is. I'm a
revivalist. You don't know what it's like
to have a feeling about your soul. I'm
terrifyingly earnest; you don't seem to
understand that. I have all the feelings
of Bunyan without his religion. I regard
the salvation of my soul as important.

How simple everything would be if one could go out with those creatures in bonnets and sing hymns like, ' Hip, hip for the blood of the Lamb, hurrah ! ' or that exquisite one :

> " ' The bells of Hell ring tingalingaling
> For you, but not for me.
> For me the angels singalingaling ;
> They've got the goods for me.'

Unhappily it's impossible."

" Your ideas," said Cravister in his flutiest voice, " are somewhat Gothic. I think I can understand them, though of course I don't sympathize or approve. My advice to people in doubt about what course of action they ought to pursue is always the same : do what you want to."

" Cravister, you're hopeless," said Dick, laughing. " I suppose I am rather Gothic, but I do feel sometimes that the question of ought as well as of want does arise."

Dick had come to his old friend for advice about Life. What ought he to do ? The indefatigable pen of Pearl Bellairs solved for him the financial problem. There remained only the moral problem : how could he best expend his energies and his time ? Should he devote himself to knowing or doing, philosophy or politics ? He felt in himself the desire to search for truth and the ability—who knows ?—to find it. On the other hand, the horrors of the world about him seemed to call on him to put forth all his strength in an effort to ameliorate what was so patently and repulsively bad. Actually, what had to be decided was this : Should he devote himself to the researches necessary to carry out the plan, long ripening in his brain, of a new system of scientific philosophy ; or should he devote his powers and Pearl Bellairs' money in propaganda that should put life into the English revolutionary movement ? Great moral principles were in the balance. And Cravister's advice was, do what you want to !

After a month of painful indecision, Dick, who was a real Englishman, arrived at a satisfactory compromise. He started work on his new Synthetic Philosophy, and at the same time joined the staff of the *Weekly International*, to which he contributed both money and articles. The weeks slipped pleasantly and profitably along. The secret of happiness lies in congenial work, and no one could have worked harder than Dick, unless it was the indefatigable Pearl Bellairs, whose nightly output of five thousand words sufficed to support not only Dick but the *Weekly International* as well. These months were perhaps the happiest period of Dick's life. He had friends, money, liberty ; he knew himself to be working well ; and it was an extra, a supererogatory happiness that he began at this time to get on much better with his sister Millicent than he had ever done before. Millicent had come up to Oxford as a student at St. Mungo Hall in Dick's third year. She had grown into a very efficient and very intelligent young woman. A particularly handsome young woman as well. She was boyishly slender, and a natural grace kept on breaking through the somewhat rigid deportment, which she always tried to impose upon herself, in little beautiful gestures and movements that made the onlooker catch his breath with astonished pleasure.

> " Wincing she was as is a jolly colt,
>   Straight as a mast and upright as a bolt : "

Chaucer had as good an eye for youthful

grace as for mormals and bristly nostrils and thick red jovial villainousness.

Millicent lost no time in making her presence at St. Mungo's felt. Second- and third-year heroines might snort at the forwardness of a mere fresh-girl, might resent the complete absence of veneration for their glory exhibited by this youthful bejauna ; Millicent pursued her course unmoved. She founded new societies and put fresh life into the institutions which already existed at St. Mungo's to take cocoa and discuss the problems of the universe. She played hockey like a tornado, and she worked alarmingly hard. Decidedly, Millicent was a Force, very soon the biggest Force in the St. Mungo world. In her fifth term she organized the famous St. Mungo general strike, which compelled the authorities to relax a few of the more intolerably tyrannical and anachronistic rules restricting the liberty of the students. It was she who went, on behalf of the strikers, to interview the redoubtable Miss Prosser, Principal of St. Mungo's. The redoubtable Miss Prosser looked grim and invited her to sit down. Millicent sat down and, without quailing, delivered a short but pointed speech attacking the fundamental principles of the St. Mungo system of discipline.

" Your whole point of view," she assured Miss Prosser, " is radically wrong. It's an insult to the female sex ; it's positively obscene. Your root assumption is simply this : that we're all in a chronic state of sexual excitement ; leave us alone for a moment and we'll immediately put our desires into practice. It's disgusting. It makes me blush. After all, Miss Prosser, we are a college of intelligent women, not an asylum of nymphomaniacs."

For the first time in her career, Miss Prosser had to admit herself beaten. The authorities gave in—reluctantly and on only a few points ; but the principle had been shaken, and that, as Millicent pointed out, was what really mattered.

Dick used to see a good deal of his sister while he was still in residence at Canteloup, and after he had gone down he used to come regularly once a fortnight during term to visit her. That horrible mutual reserve, which poisons the social life of most families and which

had effectively made of their brotherly
and sisterly relation a prolonged dis-
comfort in the past, began to disappear.
They became the best of friends.

"I like you, Dick, a great deal better
than I did," said Millicent one day as
they were parting at the gate of St.
Mungo's after a long walk together.

Dick took off his hat and bowed. "My
dear, I reciprocate the sentiment. And,
what's more, I esteem and admire you.
So there."

Millicent curtsied, and they laughed.
They both felt very happy.

V I

"WHAT a life!" said Dick, with a
sigh of weariness as the train
moved out of Euston.

Not a bad life, Millicent thought.

"But horribly fatiguing. I am quite
outreined by it."

"Outreined" was Dick's translation
of *éreinté*. He liked using words of his
own manufacture; one had to learn
his idiom before one could properly
appreciate his intimate conversation.

Dick had every justification for being outreined. The spring and summer had passed for him in a whirl of incessant activity. He had written three long chapters of the *New Synthetic Philosophy*, and had the material for two more ready in the form of notes. He had helped to organize and bring to its successful conclusion the great carpenters' strike of May and June. He had written four pamphlets and a small army of political articles. And this comprised only half his labour ; for nightly, from twelve till two, Pearl Bellairs emerged to compose the masterpieces which supplied Dick with his bread and butter. *Apes in Purple* had been published in May. Since then she had finished *La Belle Dame sans Morality*, and had embarked on the first chapters of *Daisy's Voyage to Cythera*. Her weekly articles, " For the Girls of Britain," had become, during this period, a regular and favourite feature in the pages of *Hildebrand's Sabbath*, that prince of Sunday papers. At the beginning of July, Dick considered that he had earned a holiday, and now they were off, he and Millicent, for the North.

Dick had taken a cottage on the shore of one of those long salt-water lochs that give to the west coast of Scotland such a dissipated appearance on the map. For miles around there was not a living soul who did not bear the name of Campbell—two families only excepted, one of whom was called Murray-Drummond and the other Drummond-Murray. However, it was not for the people that Dick and Millicent had come, so much as for the landscape, which made up in variety for anything that the inhabitants might lack. Behind the cottage, in the midst of a narrow strip of bog lying between the loch and the foot of the mountains, stood one of the numerous tombs of Ossian, a great barrow of ancient stones. And a couple of miles away the remains of Deirdre's Scottish refuge bore witness to the Celtic past. The countryside was dotted with the black skeletons of mediæval castles. Astonishing country, convulsed into fantastic mountain shapes, cut and indented by winding fiords. On summer days the whole of this improbable landscape became blue and remote and aerially transparent. Its beauty lacked all verisimilitude. It was for that reason that Dick chose the neighbourhood for his holidays. After the insistent actuality of London this frankly unreal coast was particularly refreshing to a jaded spirit.

" Nous sommes ici en plein romantisme," said Dick on the day of their arrival, making a comprehensive gesture towards the dream-like scenery, and for the rest of his holiday he acted the part of a young romantic of the palmy period. He sat at the foot of Ossian's tomb and read Lamartine ; he declaimed Byron from the summit of the mountains and Shelley as he rowed along the loch. In the evening he read George Sand's *Indiana* ; he agonized with the pure, but passionate, heroine, while his admiration for Sir Brown, her English lover, the impassive giant who never speaks and is always clothed in faultless hunting costume, knew no bounds. He saturated himself in the verses of Victor Hugo, and at last almost came to persuade himself that the words, *Dieu, infinité, eternité,* with which the works of that deplorable genius are so profusely sprinkled, actually possessed some meaning, though what that meaning was he could not, even in his most romantic transports, discover. Pearl Bellairs, of course, understood quite clearly their significance, and though she was a very poor French scholar she used sometimes to be moved almost to tears by the books she found lying about when she came into existence after midnight. She even copied out extracts into her notebooks with a view to using them in her next novel.

> " Les plus désespérés sont les chants les plus beaux,
> Et j'en sais d'immortels qui sont de purs sanglots,"

was a couplet which struck her as sublime.

Millicent, meanwhile, did the housekeeping with extraordinary efficiency, took a great deal of exercise, and read long, serious books ; she humoured her brother in his holiday romanticism, but refused to take part in the game.

The declaration of war took them completely by surprise. It is true that a *Scotsman* found its way into the cottage by about lunch-time every day, but it was never read, and served only to light fires and wrap up fish and things of that sort. No letters were being forwarded, for they had left no address ; they were isolated from the world. On the fatal morning Dick had, indeed, glanced at the paper, without however noticing anything out of the ordinary. It was only later when, alarmed by the rumours floating round the village shop, he came to examine his *Scotsman* more closely, that he found about half-way down the third column of one of the middle pages an admirable account of all that had been so tragically happening in the last twenty-four hours ; he learnt with horror that Europe was at war and that his country too had entered the arena. Even in the midst of his anguish of spirit he could not help admiring the *Scotsman's* splendid impassivity—no headlines, no ruffling of the traditional aristocratic dignity. Like Sir Rodolphe Brown in *Indiana*, he thought, with a sickly smile.

Dick determined to start for London at once. He felt that he must act, or at least create the illusion of action ; he could not stay quietly where he was. It was arranged that he should set out that afternoon, while Millicent should follow a day or two later with the bulk of the luggage. The train which took him to Glasgow was slower than he thought it possible for any train to be. He tried to read, he tried to sleep ; it was no good. His nervous agitation was pitiable ; he made little involuntary movements with his limbs, and every now and then the muscles of his face began twitching in a spasmodic and uncontrollable tic. There were three hours to wait in Glasgow ; he spent them in wandering about the streets. In the interminable summer twilight the inhabitants of Glasgow came forth into the open to amuse themselves ; the sight almost made him sick. Was it possible that there should be human beings so numerous and so uniformly hideous ? Small, deformed, sallow, they seemed malignantly ugly, as if on purpose. The words they spoke were incomprehensible. He shuddered ; it was an alien place—it was hell.

The London train was crammed. Three gross Italians got into Dick's carriage, and after they had drunk and eaten with loud, unpleasant gusto, they prepared themselves for sleep by taking off their

boots. Their feet smelt strongly am-
moniac, like a cage of mice long uncleaned.
Acutely awake, while the other occupants
of the compartment enjoyed a happy
unconsciousness, he looked at the huddled
carcasses that surrounded him. The
warmth and the smell of them was suffo-
cating, and there came to his mind, with
the nightmarish insistence of a fixed idea,
the thought that every breath they exhaled was saturated with disease. To
be condemned to sit in a hot bath of
consumption and syphilis—it was too
horrible ! The moment came at last
when he could bear it no longer ; he got
up and went into the corridor. Standing
there, or sitting sometimes for a few
dreary minutes in the lavatory, he passed
the rest of the night. The train roared
along without a stop. The roaring became articulate : in the days of his childhood trains used to run to the tune of
" Lancashire, to Lancashire, to fetch a
pocket-handkercher ; to Lancashire, to
Lancashire . . ." But to-night the
wheels were shouting insistently, a million
times over, two words only—" the War,
the War ; the War, the War." He tried

desperately to make them say something else, but they refused to recite Milton ; they refused to go to Lancashire ; they went on with their endless Tibetan litany— the War, the War, the War.

By the time he reached London, Dick was in a wretched state. His nerves were twittering and jumping within him ; he felt like a walking aviary. The tic in his face had become more violent and persistent. As he stood in the station, waiting for a cab, he overheard a small child saying to its mother, " What's the matter with that man's face, mother ? "

" Sh—sh, darling," was the reply. " It's rude."

Dick turned and saw the child's big round eyes fixed with fascinated curiosity upon him, as though he were a kind of monster. He put his hand to his forehead and tried to stop the twitching of the muscles beneath the skin. It pained him to think that he had become a scarecrow for children.

Arrived at his flat, Dick drank a glass of brandy and lay down for a rest. He felt exhausted—ill. At half-past one he got up, drank some more brandy, and crept down into the street. It was intensely hot ; the pavements reverberated the sunlight in a glare which hurt his eyes ; they seemed to be in a state of grey incandescence. A nauseating smell of wetted dust rose from the roadway, along which a water-cart was slowly piddling its way. He realized suddenly that he ought not to have drunk all that brandy on an empty stomach ; he was definitely rather tipsy. He had arrived at that state of drunkenness when the senses perceive things clearly, but do not transmit their knowledge to the understanding. He was painfully conscious of this division, and it needed all the power of his will to establish contact between his parted faculties. It was as though he were, by a great and prolonged effort, keeping his brain pressed against the back of his eyes ; as soon as he relaxed the pressure, the understanding part slipped back, the contact was broken, and he relapsed into a state bordering on imbecility. The actions which ordinarily one does by habit and without thinking, he had to perform consciously and voluntarily. He had to reason out the problem of walking—first the left foot

5

forward, then the right. How ingeniously he worked his ankles and knees and hips! How delicately the thighs slid past one another!

He found a restaurant and sat there drinking coffee and trying to eat an omelette until he felt quite sober. Then he drove to the offices of the *Weekly International* to have a talk with Hyman, the editor. Hyman was sitting in his shirt-sleeves, writing.

He lifted his head as Dick came in. " Greenow," he shouted delightedly, " we were all wondering what had become of you. We thought you'd joined the Army."

Dick shook his head, but did not speak; the hot stuffy smell of printer's ink and machinery combined with the atrocious reek of Hyman's Virginian cigarettes to make him feel rather faint. He sat down on the window-ledge, so as to be able to breathe an uncontaminated air.

" Well," he said at last, " what about it ? "

" It's going to be hell."

" Did you suppose I thought it was going to be paradise ? " Dick replied irritably. " Internationalism looks rather funny now, doesn't it ? "

" I believe in it more than ever I did," cried Hyman. His face lit up with the fervour of his enthusiasm. It was a fine face, gaunt, furrowed, and angular, for all that he was barely thirty, looking as though it had been boldly chiselled from some hard stone. " The rest of the world may go mad ; we'll try and keep our sanity. The time will come when they'll see we were right."

Hyman talked on. His passionate sincerity and singleness of purpose were an inspiration to Dick. He had always admired Hyman—with the reservations, of course, that the man was rather a fanatic and not so well-educated as he might have been—but to-day he admired him more than ever. He was even moved by that perhaps too facile eloquence which of old had been used to leave him cold. After promising to do a series of articles on international relations for the paper, Dick went home, feeling better than he had done all day.

He decided that he would begin writing his articles at once. He collected pens.

paper, and ink and sat down in a business-like way at his bureau. He remembered distinctly biting the tip of his pen-holder ; it tasted rather bitter.

And then he realized he was standing in Regent Street, looking in at one of the windows of Liberty's.

For a long time he stood there quite still, absorbed to all appearance in the contemplation of a piece of peacock-blue fabric. But all his attention was concentrated within himself, not on anything outside. He was wondering—wondering how it came about that he was sitting at his writing-table at one moment, and standing, at the next, in Regent Street. He hadn't—the thought flashed upon him —he hadn't been drinking any more of that brandy, had he ? No, he felt himself to be perfectly sober. He moved slowly away and continued to speculate as he walked.

At Oxford Circus he bought an evening paper. He almost screamed aloud when he saw that the date printed at the head of the page was August 12th. It was on August 7th that he had sat down at his writing-table to compose those articles.

Five days ago, and he had not the faintest recollection of what had happened in those five days.

He made all haste back to the flat. Everything was in perfect order. He had evidently had a picnic lunch that morning —sardines, bread and jam, and raisins ; the remains of it still covered the table. He opened the sideboard and took out the brandy bottle. Better make quite sure. He held it up to the light ; it was more than three-quarters full. Not a drop had gone since the day of his return. If brandy wasn't the cause, then what was ?

As he sat there thinking, he began in an absent-minded way to look at his evening paper. He read the news on the front page, then turned to the inner sheets. His eye fell on these words printed at the head of the column next the leading article :

" To the Women of the Empire. Thoughts in War-Time. By Pearl Bellairs." Underneath in brackets : " The first of a series of inspiring patriotic articles by Miss Bellairs, the well-known novelist."

Dick groaned in agony. He saw in a

flash what had happened to his five missing days. Pearl had got hold of them somehow, had trespassed upon his life out of her own reserved nocturnal existence. She had taken advantage of his agitated mental state to have a little fun in her own horrible way.

He picked up the paper once more and began to read Pearl's article. " Inspiring and patriotic " : those were feeble words in which to describe Pearl's shrilly raucous chauvinism. And the style ! Christ ! to think that he was responsible, at least in part, for this. Responsible, for had not the words been written by his own hand and composed in some horrible bluebeard's chamber of his own brain ? They had, there was no denying it. Pearl's literary atrocities had never much distressed him ; he had long given up reading a word she wrote. Her bank balance was the only thing about her that interested him. But now she was invading the sanctities of his private life. She was trampling on his dearest convictions, denying his faith. She was a public danger. It was all too frightful.

He passed the afternoon in misery. Suicide or brandy seemed the only cures. Not very satisfactory ones, though. Towards evening an illuminating idea occurred to him. He would go and see Rogers. Rogers knew all about psychology—from books, at any rate : Freud, Jung, Morton Prince, and people like that. He used to try hypnotic experiments on his friends and even dabbled in amateur psychotherapy. Rogers might help him to lay the ghost of Pearl. He ate a hasty dinner and went to see Rogers in his Kensington rooms.

Rogers was sitting at a table with a great book open in front of him. The reading-lamp, which was the only light in the room, brightly illumined one side of the pallid, puffy, spectacled face, leaving the other in complete darkness, save for a little cedilla of golden light caught on the fold of flesh at the corner of his mouth. His huge shadow crossed the floor, began to climb the wall, and from the shoulders upwards mingled itself with the general darkness of the room.

" Good evening, Rogers," said Dick

wearily. "I wish you wouldn't try and look like Rembrandt's 'Christ at Emmaus' with these spectacular chiaroscuro effects."

Rogers gave vent to his usual nervous giggling laugh. "This is very nice of you to come and see me, Greenow."

"How's the Board of Trade?" Rogers was a Civil Servant by profession.

"Oh, business as usual, as the *Daily Mail* would say." Rogers laughed again as though he had made a joke.

After a little talk of things indifferent, Dick brought the conversation round to himself.

"I believe I'm getting a bit neurasthenic," he said. "Fits of depression, nervous pains, lassitude, anæmia of the will. I've come to you for professional advice. I want you to nose out my suppressed complexes, analyse me, dissect me. Will you do that for me?"

Rogers was evidently delighted. "I'll do my best," he said, with assumed modesty. "But I'm no good at the thing, so you mustn't expect much."

"I'm at your disposal," said Dick.

Rogers placed his guest in a large arm-chair. "Relax your muscles and think of nothing at all." Dick sat there flabby and abstracted while Rogers made his preparations. His apparatus consisted chiefly in a notebook and a stop-watch. He seated himself at the table.

"Now," he said solemnly, "I want you to listen to me. I propose to read out a list of words; after each of the words you must say the first word that comes into your head. The very first, mind, however foolish it may seem. And say it as soon as it crosses your mind; don't wait to think. I shall write down your answers and take the time between each question and reply."

Rogers cleared his throat and started.

"Mother," he said in a loud, clear voice. He always began his analyses with the family. For since the majority of kinks and complexes date from childhood, it is instructive to investigate the relations between the patient and those who surrounded him at an early age. "Mother."

"Dead," replied Dick immediately. He had scarcely known his mother.

"Father."

" Dull." One and a fifth seconds' interval.

" Sister." Rogers pricked his ears for the reply : his favourite incest-theory depended on it.

" Fabian Society," said Dick, after two seconds' interval. Rogers was a little disappointed. He was agreeably thrilled and excited by the answer he received to his next word : " Aunt."

The seconds passed, bringing nothing with them ; and then at last there floated into Dick's mind the image of himself as a child, dressed in green velvet and lace, a perfect Bubbles boy, kneeling on Auntie Loo's lap and arranging a troop of lead soldiers on the horizontal projection of her corsage.

" Bosom," he said.

Rogers wrote down the word and underlined it. Six and three-fifths seconds : very significant. He turned now to the chapter of possible accidents productive of nervous shocks.

" Fire."

" Coal."

" Sea."

" Sick."

" Train."

" Smell."

And so on. Dull answers all the time. Evidently, nothing very catastrophic had ever happened to him. Now for a frontal attack on the fortress of sex itself.

" Women." There was rather a long pause, four seconds, and then Dick replied, " Novelist." Rogers was puzzled.

" Breast."

" Chicken." That was disappointing. Rogers could find no trace of those sinister moral censors, expurgators of impulse, suppressors of happiness. Perhaps the trouble lay in religion.

" Christ," he said.

Dick replied, " Amen," with the promptitude of a parish clerk.

" God."

Dick's mind remained a perfect blank. The word seemed to convey to him nothing at all. God, God. After a long time there appeared before his inward eye the face of a boy he had known at school and at Oxford, one Godfrey Wilkinson, called God for short.

" Wilkinson." Ten seconds and a fifth.

A few more miscellaneous questions, and the list was exhausted. Almost suddenly, Dick fell into a kind of hypnotic sleep. Rogers sat pensive in front of his notes ; sometimes he consulted a text-book. At the end of half an hour he awakened Dick to tell him that he had had, as a child, consciously or unconsciously, a great Freudian passion for his aunt ; that later on he had had another passion, almost religious in its fervour and intensity, for somebody called Wilkinson ; and that the cause of all his present troubles lay in one or other of these episodes. If he liked, he (Rogers) would investigate the matter further with a view to establishing a cure.

Dick thanked him very much, thought it wasn't worth taking any more trouble, and went home.

VII

MILLICENT was organizing a hospital supply dépôt, organizing indefatigably, from morning till night. It was October ; Dick had not seen his sister since those first hours of the war in Scotland ; he had had too much to think about these last months to pay attention to anyone but himself. To-day, at last, he decided that he would go and pay her a visit. Millicent had commandeered a large house in Kensington from a family of Jews, who were anxious to live down a deplorable name by a display of patriotism. Dick found her sitting there in her office— young, formidable, beautiful, severe—at a big desk covered with papers.

" Well," said Dick, " you're winning the war, I see."

" You, I gather, are not," Millicent replied.

" I believe in the things I always believed in."

" So do I."

" But in a different way, my dear—in a different way," said Dick sadly. There was a silence.

" Had we better quarrel ? " Millicent asked meditatively.

" I think we can manage with nothing worse than a coolness—for the duration."

" Very well, a coolness."

" A smouldering coolness."

" Good," said Millicent briskly. "Let
it start smouldering at once I must get
on with my work. Good-bye, Dick. God
bless you. Let me know sometimes how
you get on."

" No need to ask how you get on," said
Dick with a smile, as he shook her hand.
" I know by experience that you always
get on, only too well, ruthlessly well."

He went out. Millicent returned to her
letters with concentrated ardour ; a frown
puckered the skin between her eyebrows.

Probably, Dick reflected as he made his
way down the stairs, he wouldn't see her
again for a year or so. He couldn't
honestly say that it affected him much.
Other people became daily more and more
like ghosts, unreal, thin, vaporous ; while
every hour the consciousness of himself
grew more intense and all-absorbing.
The only person who was more than a
shadow to him now was Hyman of the
Weekly International. In those first
horrible months of the war, when he was
wrestling with Pearl Bellairs and failing to
cast her out, it was Hyman who kept him
from melancholy and suicide. Hyman
made him write a long article every week,

dragged him into the office to do sub-
editorial work, kept him so busy that there
were long hours when he had no time to
brood over his own insoluble problems.
And his enthusiasm was so passionate and
sincere that sometimes even Dick was
infected by it ; he could believe that life
was worth living and the cause worth
fighting for. But not for long ; for the
devil would return, insistent and untiring.
Pearl Bellairs was greedy for life ; she was
not content with her short midnight hours ;
she wanted the freedom of whole days.
And whenever Dick was overtired, or ill or
nervous, she leapt upon him and stamped
him out of existence, till enough strength
came back for him to reassert his person-
ality. And the articles she wrote ! The
short stories ! The recruiting songs !
Dick dared not read them ; they were
terrible, terrible.

VIII

THE months passed by. The longer
the war lasted, the longer it seemed
likely to last. Dick supported life somehow. Then came the menace of conscrip-

tion. The *Weekly International* organized
a great anti-conscription campaign, in
which Hyman and Dick were the leading
spirits. Dick was almost happy. This
kind of active work was new to him and
he enjoyed it, finding it exciting and at
the same time sedative. For a self-ab-
sorbed and brooding mind, pain itself is
an anodyne. He enjoyed his incessant
journeys, his speechmaking to queer
audiences in obscure halls and chapels ;
he liked talking with earnest members of
impossible Christian sects, pacifists who
took not the faintest interest in the welfare
of humanity at large, but were wholly
absorbed in the salvation of their own
souls and in keeping their consciences clear
from the faintest trace of blood-guiltiness.
He enjoyed the sense of power which came
to him, when he roused the passion of the
crowd to enthusiastic assent, or breasted
the storm of antagonism. He enjoyed
everything—even getting a bloody nose
from a patriot hired and intoxicated by a
great evening paper to break up one of his
meetings. It all seemed tremendously
exciting and important at the time. And
yet when, in quiet moments, he came

to look back on his days of activity, they seemed utterly empty and futile. What was left of them ? Nothing, nothing at all. The momentary intoxication had died away, the stirred ant's-nest had gone back to normal life. Futility of action : There was nothing permanent, or decent, or worth while, except thought. And of that he was almost incapable now. His mind, when it was not occupied by the immediate and actual, turned inward morbidly upon itself. He looked at the manuscript of his book and wondered whether he would ever be able to go on with it. It seemed doubtful. Was he, then, condemned to pass the rest of his existence enslaved to the beastliness and futility of mere quotidian action ? And even in action his powers were limited ; if he exerted himself too much—and the limits of fatigue were soon reached— Pearl Bellairs, watching perpetually like a hungry tigress for her opportunity, leapt upon him and took possession of his conscious faculties. And then, it might be for a matter of hours or of days, he was lost, blotted off the register of living souls, while she performed, with intense and

6

hideous industry, her self-appointed task. More than once his anti-conscription campaigns had been cut short and he himself had suddenly disappeared from public life, to return with the vaguest stories of illness or private affairs—stories that made his friends shake their heads and wonder which it was among the noble army of vices that poor Dick Greenow was so mysteriously addicted to. Some said drink, some said women, some said opium, and some hinted at things infinitely darker and more horrid. Hyman asked him point-blank what it was, one morning when he had returned to the office after three days' unaccountable absence.

Dick blushed painfully. " It isn't anything you think," he said.

" What is it, then ? " Hyman insisted.

" I can't tell you," Dick replied desperately and in torture, " but I swear it's nothing discreditable. I beg you won't ask me any more."

Hyman had to pretend to be satisfied with that.

IX

A TACTICAL move in the anti-conscription campaign was the foundation of a club, a place where people with pacific or generally advanced ideas could congregate.

" A club like this would soon be the intellectual centre of London," said Hyman, ever sanguine.

Dick shrugged his shoulders. He had a wide experience of pacifists.

" If you bring people together," Hyman went on, " they encourage one another to be bold — strengthen one another's faith."

" Yes," said Dick dyspeptically. " When they're in a herd, they can believe that they're much more numerous and important than they really are."

" But, man, they are numerous, they are important ! " Hyman shouted and gesticulated.

Dick allowed himself to be persuaded into an optimism which he knew to be ill-founded. The consolations of religion

do not console the less efficaciously for
being illusory.

It was a long time before they could think
of a suitable name for their club. Dick
suggested that it should be called the
Sclopis Club. "Such a lovely name," he
explained. "Sclopis—Sclopis; it tastes
precious in the mouth." But the rest of
the committee would not hear of it;
they wanted a name that meant something. One lady suggested that it should be
called the Everyman Club; Dick objected
with passion. "It makes one shudder,"
he said. The lady thought it was a
beautiful and uplifting name, but as Mr.
Greenow was so strongly opposed, she
wouldn't press the claims of Everyman.
Hyman wanted to call it the Pacifist
Club, but that was judged too provocative.
Finally, they agreed to call it the Nov-
embrist Club, because it was November
and they could think of no better title.

The inaugural dinner of the Novem-
brist Club was held at Piccolomini's
Restaurant. Piccolomini is in, but not
exactly of, Soho, for it is a cross between
a Soho restaurant and a Corner House, a
hybrid which combines the worst quali-

ties of both parents—the dirt and in-
efficiency of Soho, the size and vulgarity of
Lyons. There is a large upper chamber
reserved for agapes. Here, one wet and
dismal winter's evening, the Novembrists
assembled.

Dick arrived early, and from his place
near the door he watched his fellow-
members come in. He didn't much like
the look of them. " Middle class " was
what he found himself thinking; and he
had to admit, when his conscience re-
proached him for it, that he did not like
the middle classes, the lower middle classes,
the lower classes. He was, there was no
denying it, a bloodsucker at heart—
cultured and intelligent, perhaps, but a
bloodsucker none the less.

The meal began. Everything about it
was profoundly suspect. The spoons were
made of some pale pinchbeck metal, very
light and flimsy; one expected them to
melt in the soup, or one would have done, if
the soup had been even tepid. The food
was thick and greasy. Dick wondered
what it really looked like under the con-
cealing sauces. The wine left an inde-
scribable taste that lingered on the palate,

like the savour of brass or of charcoal fumes.

From childhood upwards Dick had suffered from the intensity of his visceral reactions to emotion. Fear and shyness were apt to make him feel very sick, and disgust produced in him a sensation of intolerable queasiness. Disgust had seized upon his mind to-night. He grew paler with the arrival of every dish, and the wine, instead of cheering him, made him feel much worse. His neighbours to right and left ate with revolting heartiness. On one side sat Miss Gibbs, garishly dressed in ill-assorted colours that might be called futuristic ; on the other was Mr. Something in pince-nez, rather ambrosial about the hair. Mr. Something was a poet, or so the man who introduced them had said. Miss Gibbs was just an ordinary member of the Intelligentsia, like the rest of us.

The Lower Classes, the Lower Classes . . .

" Are you interested in the Modern Theatre ? " asked Mr. Something in his mellow voice. Too mellow—oh, much too mellow !

" Passably," said Dick.

" So am I," said Mr. Thingummy. " I am a vice-president of the Craftsmen's League of Joy, which perhaps you may have heard of."

Dick shook his head ; this was going to be terrible.

" The objects of the Craftsmen's League of Joy," Mr. Thingummy continued, " or rather, one of the objects— for it has many—is to establish Little Theatres in every town and village in England, where simple, uplifting, beautiful plays might be acted. The people have no joy."

" They have the cinema and the music hall," said Dick. He was filled with a sudden senseless irritation. " They get all the joy they want out of the jokes of the comics and the legs of the women."

" Ah, but that is an impure joy," Mr. What's-his-name protested.

" Impure purple, Herbert Spenser's favourite colour," flashed irrelevantly through Dick's brain.

" Well, speaking for myself," he said aloud, " I know I get more joy out of a good pair of legs than out of any number of uplifting plays of the kind they'd be sure to act in your little theatres. The people ask for sex and you give them a stone."

How was it, he wondered, that the right opinions in the mouths of these people sounded so horribly cheap and wrong ? They degraded what was noble ; beauty became fly-blown at their touch. Their intellectual tradition was all wrong. Lower classes, it always came back to that. When they talked about war and the International, Dick felt a hot geyser of chauvinism bubbling up in his breast. In order to say nothing stupid, he refrained from speaking at all. Miss Gibbs switched the conversation on to art. She admired all the right people. Dick told her that he thought Sir Luke Fildes to be the best modern artist. But his irritation knew no bounds when he found out a little later that Mr. Something had read the poems of Fulke Greville, Lord Brooke. He felt inclined to say, " You may have read them, but of course you can't understand or appreciate them."

Lower Classes . . .

How clear and splendid were the ideas of right and justice ! If only one could filter away the contaminating human element. . . . Reason compelled him to believe in democracy, in international- ism, in revolution ; morality demanded justice for the oppressed. But neither morality nor reason would ever bring him to take pleasure in the company of demo- crats or revolutionaries, or make him find the oppressed, individually, any less antipathetic.

At the end of this nauseating meal, Dick was called on to make a speech. Rising to his feet, he began stammering and hesitating ; he felt like an imbecile. Then suddenly inspiration came. The great religious ideas of Justice and Demo- cracy swept like a rushing wind through his mind, purging it of all insignificant human and personal preferences or dis- likes. He was filled with pentecostal fire. He spoke in a white heat of in- tellectual passion, dominating his hearers, infecting them with his own high enthusi- asm. He sat down amid cheers. Miss Gibbs and Mr. Thingummy leaned towards him with flushed, shining faces.

" That was wonderful, Mr. Greenow. I've never heard anything like it," exclaimed Miss Gibbs, with genuine, unflattering enthusiasm.

Mr. Thing said something poetical about a trumpet-call. Dick looked from one to the other with blank and fishy eyes. So it was for these creatures he had been speaking!

Good God! . . .

X

DICK'S life was now a monotonous nightmare. The same impossible situation was repeated again and again. If it were not for the fact that he knew Pearl Bellairs to be entirely devoid of humour, Dick might have suspected that she was having a little quiet fun with him, so grotesque were the anomalies of his double life. Grotesque, but dreary, intolerably dreary. Situations which seem, in contemplation, romantic and adventurous have a habit of proving, when actually experienced, as dull and daily as a bank clerk's routine. When you read about it, a Jekyll and Hyde existence sounds delightfully amusing; but when you live through it, as Dick found to his cost, it is merely a boring horror.

In due course Dick was called up by the Military Authorities. He pleaded conscientious objection. The date of his appearance before the Tribunal was fixed. Dick did not much relish the prospect of being a Christian martyr; it seemed an anachronism. However, it would have to be done. He would be an absolutist; there would be a little buffeting, spitting, and scourging, followed by an indefinite term of hard labour. It was all very unpleasant. But nothing could be much more unpleasant than life as he was now living it. He didn't even mind very much if they killed him. Being or not being—the alternatives left him equally cold.

The days that preceded his appearance before the Tribunal were busy days, spent in consulting solicitors, preparing speeches, collecting witnesses.

"We'll give you a good run for your money," said Hyman. "I hope they'll be feeling a little uncomfortable by the time they have done with you, Greenow."

"Not nearly so uncomfortable as I

shall be feeling," Dick replied, with a slightly melancholy smile.

The South Marylebone Tribunal sat in a gloomy and fetid chamber in a police station. Dick, who was extremely sensitive to his surroundings, felt his fatigue and nervousness perceptibly increase as he entered the room. Five or six pitiable creatures with paralytic mothers or one-man businesses were briskly disposed of, and then it was Dick's turn to present himself before his judges. He looked round the court, nodded to Hyman, smiled at Millicent, who had so far thawed their wartime coolness as to come and see him condemned, caught other friendly eyes. It was as though he were about to be electrocuted. The preliminaries passed off; he found himself answering questions in a loud, clear voice. Then the Military Representative began to loom horribly large. The Military Representative was a solicitor's clerk disguised as a lieutenant in the Army Service Corps. He spoke in an accent that was more than genteel; it was rich, noble, aristocratic. Dick tried to remember where he had heard a man speaking like that before. He had it now. Once when he had been at Oxford after term was over. He had gone to see the Varieties, which come twice nightly and with cheap seats to the theatre after the undergraduates have departed. One of the turns had been a Nut, a descendant of the bloods and Champagne Charlies of earlier days. A young man in an alpaca evening suit and a monocle. He had danced, sung a song, spoken some patter. Sitting in the front row of the stalls, Dick had been able to see the large, swollen, tuberculous glands in his neck. They wobbled when he danced or sang. Fascinatingly horrible, those glands; and the young man, how terribly, painfully pathetic. . . . When the Military Representative spoke, he could hear again that wretched Nut's rendering of the Eton and Oxford voice. It unnerved him.

"What is your religion, Mr. Greenow?" the Military Representative asked.

Fascinated, Dick looked to see whether he too had tuberculous glands. The Lieutenant had to repeat his question sharply. When he was irritated, his voice went back to its more natural nasal twang. Dick recovered his presence of mind.

" I have no religion," he answered.

" But, surely, sir, you must have some kind of religion."

" Well, if I must, if it's in the Army Regulations, you had better put me down as an Albigensian, or a Bogomile, or, better still, as a Manichean. One can't find oneself in this court without possessing a profound sense of the reality and active existence of a power of evil equal to, if not greater than, the power of good."

" This is rather irrelevant, Mr. Greenow," said the Chairman.

" I apologize." Dick bowed to the court.

" But if," the Military Representative continued—" if your objection is not religious, may I ask what it is ? "

" It is based on a belief that all war is wrong, and that the solidarity of the human race can only be achieved in practice by protesting against war, wherever it appears and in whatever form."

" Do you disbelieve in force, Mr.
Greenow ? "

" You might as well ask me if I disbelieve in gravitation. Of course, I
believe in force : it is a fact."

" What would you do if you saw a
German violating your sister ? " said
the Military Representative, putting his
deadliest question.

" Perhaps I had better ask my sister
first," Dick replied.   " She is sitting just
behind you in the court."

The Military Representative was
covered with confusion. He coughed
and blew his nose.   The case dragged on.
Dick made a speech ; the Military Representative made a speech ; the Chairman made a speech. The atmosphere
of the court-room grew fouler and fouler.
Dick sickened and suffocated in the
second-hand air. An immense lassitude
took possession of him ; he did not care
about anything—about the cause, about
himself, about Hyman or Millicent or
Pearl Bellairs. He was just tired.
Voices buzzed and drawled in his ears
—sometimes his own voice, sometimes
other people's. He did not listen to

what they said. He was tired—tired of all this idiotic talk, tired of the heat and smell. . . .

Tired of picking up very thistly wheat sheaves and propping them up in stooks on the yellow stubble. For that was what, suddenly, he found himself doing. Overhead the sky expanded in endless steppes of blue-hot cobalt. The pungent prickly dust of the dried sheaves plucked at his nose with imminent sneezes, made his eyes smart and water. In the distance a reaping-machine whirred and hummed. Dick looked blankly about him, wondering where he was. He was thankful, at any rate, not to be in that sweltering court-room ; and it was a mercy, too, to have escaped from the odious gentility of the Military Representative's accent. And, after all, there were worse occupations than harvesting.

Gradually, and bit by bit, Dick pieced together his history. He had, it seemed, done a cowardly and treacherous thing : deserted in the face of the enemy, be-trayed his cause. He had a bitter letter from Hyman. " Why couldn't you have stuck it out ? I thought it was in you. You've urged others to go to prison for their beliefs, but you get out of it yourself by sneaking off to a soft alternative service job on a friend's estate. You've brought discredit on the whole movement." It was very painful, but what could he answer ? The truth was so ridiculous that nobody could be expected to swallow it. And yet the fact was that he had been as much startled to find himself working at Crome as anyone. It was all Pearl's doing.

He had found in his room a piece of paper covered with the large, flamboyant feminine writing which he knew to be Pearl's. It was evidently the rough copy of an article on the delights of being a land-girl: dewy dawns, rosy children's faces, quaint cottages, mossy thatch, milkmaids, healthy exercise. Pearl was being a land-girl ; but he could hardly explain the fact to Hyman. Better not attempt to answer him.

Dick hated the manual labour of the farm. It was hard, monotonous, dirty, and depressing. It inhibited almost com-

7

pletely the functions of his brain. He was unable to think about anything at all; there was no opportunity to do anything but feel uncomfortable. God had not made him a Caliban to scatter ordure over fields, to pick up ordure from cattle-yards. His rôle was Prospero.

" Ban, Ban, Caliban "—it was to that derisive measure that he pumped water, sawed wood, mowed grass; it was a march for his slow, clotted feet as he followed the dung-carts up the winding lanes. " Ban, Ban, Caliban—Ban, Ban, Ban . . ."

" Oh, that bloody old fool Tolstoy," was his profoundest reflection on a general subject in three months of manual labour and communion with mother earth.

He hated the work, and his fellow-workers hated him. They mistrusted him because they could not understand him, taking the silence of his overpowering shyness for arrogance and the contempt of one class for another. Dick longed to become friendly with them. His chief trouble was that he did not know what to say. At meal-times he would spend long minutes in cudgelling his brains for some suitable remark to make. And even if he thought of something good, like—" It looks as though it were going to be a good year for roots," he somehow hesitated to speak, feeling that such a remark, uttered in his exquisitely modulated tones, would be, somehow, a little ridiculous. It was the sort of thing that ought to be said rustically, with plenty of Z's and long vowels, in the manner of William Barnes. In the end, for lack of courage to act the yokel's part, he generally remained silent. While the others were eating their bread and cheese with laughter and talk, he sat like the skeleton at the feast—a skeleton that longed to join in the revelry, but had not the power to move its stony jaws. On the rare occasions that he actually succeeded in uttering something, the labourers looked at one another in surprise and alarm, as though it were indeed a skeleton that had spoken.

He was not much more popular with the other inhabitants of the village. Often, in the evenings, as he was returning from work, the children would pursue him, yelling. With the unerringly cruel instinct of the young they had recognized in him a fit object for abuse and lapidation.

An outcast member of another class, from whom that class in casting him out had withdrawn its protection, an alien in speech and habit, a criminal, as their zealous schoolmaster lost no opportunity of reminding them, guilty of the blackest treason against God and man—he was the obviously predestined victim of childish persecution. When stones began to fly, and dung and precocious obscenity, he bowed his head and pretended not to notice that anything unusual was happening. It was difficult, however, to look quite dignified.

There were occasional short alleviations to the dreariness of his existence. One day, when he was engaged in his usual occupation of manuring, a familiar figure suddenly appeared along the footpath through the field. It was Mrs. Cravister. She was evidently staying at the big house; one of the Manorial dachshunds preceded her. He took off his cap.

"Mr. Greenow!" she exclaimed, coming to a halt. "Ah, what a pleasure to see you again! Working on the land: so Tolstoyan. But I trust it doesn't affect your æsthetic ideas in the same way as it did his. Fifty peasants singing together is music ; but Bach's chromatic fantasia is mere gibbering incomprehensibility."

" I don't do this for pleasure," Dick explained. " It's hard labour, meted out to the Conscientious Objector."

" Of course, of course," said Mrs. Cravister, raising her hand to arrest any further explanation. " I had forgotten. A conscientious objector, a Bible student. I remember how passionately devoted you were, even at school, to the Bible."

She closed her eyes and nodded her head several times.

" On the contrary——" Dick began ; but it was no good. Mrs. Cravister had determined that he should be a Bible student and it was no use gainsaying her. She cut him short.

" Dear me, the Bible. . . . What a style ! That alone would prove it to have been directly inspired. You remember how Mahomet appealed to the beauty of his style as a sign of his divine mission. Why has nobody done the same for the Bible ? It remains for you, Mr. Greenow, to do so. You will

write a book about it. How I envy
you ! "

" The style is very fine," Dick ventured,
" but don't you think the matter occasionally leaves something to be desired ? "

" The matter is nothing," cried Mrs.
Cravister, making a gesture that seemed
to send all meaning flying like a pinch of
salt along the wind—" nothing at all.
It's the style that counts. Think of
Madame Bovary."

" I certainly will," said Dick.

Mrs. Cravister held out her hand.
" Good-bye. Yes, I certainly envy you.
I envy you your innocent labour and
your incessant study of that most
wonderful of books. If I were asked,
Mr. Greenow, what book I should take
with me to a desert island, what single
solitary book, I should certainly say the
Bible, though, indeed, there are moments
when I think I should choose *Tristram
Shandy*. Good-bye."

Mrs. Cravister sailed slowly away.
The little brown basset trotted ahead,
straining his leash. One had the impression of a great ship being towed
into harbour by a diminutive tug.

Dick was cheered by this glimpse of civilization and humanity. The unexpected arrival, one Saturday afternoon, of Millicent was not quite such an unmixed pleasure. "I've come to see how you're getting on," she announced, "and to put your cottage straight and make you comfortable."

"Very kind of you," said Dick. He didn't want his cottage put straight.

Millicent was in the Ministry of Munitions now, controlling three thousand female clerks with unsurpassed efficiency. Dick looked at her curiously, as she talked that evening of her doings. "To think I should have a sister like that," he said to himself. She was terrifying.

"You do enjoy bullying other people!" he exclaimed at last. "You've found your true vocation. One sees now how the new world will be arranged after the war. The women will continue to do all the bureaucratic jobs, all that entails routine and neatness and interfering with other people's affairs. And man, it is to be hoped, will be left free for the important statesman's business, free for creation and thought. He will stay at home and give proper education to the children, too. He is fit to do these things, because his mind is disinterested and detached. It's an arrangement which will liberate all man's best energies for their proper uses. The only flaw I can see in the system is that you women will be so fiendishly and ruthlessly tyrannical in your administration."

" You can't seriously expect me to argue with you," said Millicent.

" No, please don't. I am not strong enough. My dung-carrying has taken the edge off all my reasoning powers."

Millicent spent the next morning in completely rearranging Dick's furniture. By lunch-time every article in the cottage was occupying a new position.

" That's much nicer," said Millicent, surveying her work and seeing that it was good.

There was a knock at the door. Dick opened it and was astonished to find Hyman.

" I just ran down to see how you were getting on," he explained.

" I'm getting on very well since my sister rearranged my furniture," said Dick. He found it pleasing to have an opportunity of exercising his long un-used powers of malicious irony. This was very mild, but with practice he would soon come on to something more spiteful and amusing.

Hyman shook hands with Millicent, scowling as he did so. He was irritated that she was there ; he wanted to talk with Dick alone. He turned his back on her and began addressing Dick.

" Well," he said, " I haven't seen you since the fatal day. How is the turnip-hoeing ? "

" Pretty beastly," said Dick.

" Better than doing hard labour in a gaol, I suppose ? "

Dick nodded his head wearily, fore-seeing what must inevitably come.

" You've escaped that all right," Hyman went on.

" Yes ; you ought to be thankful," Millicent chimed in.

" I still can't understand why you did it, Greenow. It was a blow to me. I didn't expect it of you." Hyman spoke with feeling. "It was desertion; it was treason."

"I agree," said Millicent judicially. "He ought to have stuck to his principles."

"He ought to have stuck to what was right, oughtn't he, Miss Greenow?" Hyman turned towards Millicent, pleased at finding someone who shared his views.

"Of course," she replied—"of course. I totally disagree with you about what is right. But if he believed it right not to fight, he certainly ought to have gone to prison for his belief."

Dick lit a pipe with an air of nonchalance. He tried to disguise the fact that he was feeling extremely uncomfortable under these two pairs of merciless, accusing eyes.

"To my mind, at any rate," said Millicent, "your position seems quite illogical and untenable, Dick."

It was a relief to be talked to and not about.

"I'm sorry about that," said Dick rather huskily—not a very intelligent remark, but what was there to say?

"Of course, it's illogical and untenable.

Your sister is quite right." Hyman banged the table.

"I can't understand what induced you to take it up——"

"After you'd said you were going to be one of the absolutes," cried Hyman, interrupting and continuing Millicent's words.

"Why ? " said Millicent.

"Why, why, why ? " Hyman echoed.

Dick, who had been blowing out smoke at a great rate, put down his pipe. The taste of the tobacco was making him feel rather sick. "I wish you would stop," he said wearily. "If I gave you the real reasons, you wouldn't believe me. And I can't invent any others that would be in the least convincing."

"I believe the real reason is that you were afraid of prison."

Dick leaned back in his chair and shut his eyes. He did not mind being insulted now ; it made no difference. Hyman and Millicent were still talking about him, but what they said did not interest him ; he scarcely listened.

They went back to London together in the evening.

"Very intelligent woman, your sister," said Hyman just before they were starting. "Pity she's not on the right side about the war and so forth."

Four weeks later Dick received a letter in which Hyman announced that he and Millicent had decided to get married.

"I am happy to think," Dick wrote in his congratulatory reply, "that it was I who brought you together."

He smiled as he read through the sentence; that was what the Christian martyr might say to the two lions who had scraped acquaintance over his bones in the amphitheatre.

One warm afternoon in the summer of 1918, Mr. Hobart, Clerk to the Wibley Town Council, was disturbed in the midst of his duties by the sudden entry into his office of a small dark man, dressed in corduroys and gaiters, but not having the air of a genuine agricultural labourer.

"What may I do for you?" inquired Mr. Hobart.

"I have come to inquire about my vote," said the stranger.

"Aren't you already registered?"

" Not yet.   You see, it isn't long since the Act was passed giving us the vote."

Mr. Hobart stared.

" I don't quite follow," he said.

" I may not look it," said the stranger, putting his head on one side and looking arch—" I may not look it, but I will confess to you, Mr.—er—Mr.—er—— "

" Hobart."

" Mr. Hobart, that I am a woman of over thirty."

Mr. Hobart grew visibly paler.   Then, assuming a forced smile and speaking as one speaks to a child or a spoiled animal, he said :

" I see — I see.   Over thirty, dear me."

He looked at the bell, which was over by the fireplace at the other side of the room, and wondered how he should ring it without rousing the maniac's suspicions.

" Over thirty," the stranger went on. " You know my woman's secret.   I am Miss Pearl Bellairs, the novelist.   Perhaps you have read some of my books.   Or are you too busy ? "

" Oh no, I've read several," Mr. Hobart replied, smiling more and more brightly and speaking in even more coaxing and indulgent tones.

"Then we're friends already, Mr. Hobart. Anyone who knows my books, knows me. My whole heart is in them. Now, you must tell me all about my poor little vote. I shall be very patriotic with it when the time comes to use it."

Mr. Hobart saw his opportunity.

"Certainly, Miss Bellairs," he said. "I will ring for my clerk and we'll—er —we'll take down the details."

He got up, crossed the room, and rang the bell with violence.

"I'll just go and see that he brings the right books," he added, and darted to the door. Once outside in the passage, he mopped his face and heaved a sigh of relief. That had been a narrow shave, by Jove. A loony in the office—dangerous-looking brute, too.

On the following day Dick woke up and found himself in a bare whitewashed room, sparsely furnished with a little iron bed, a washstand, a chair, and table. He looked round him in surprise. Where had he got to this time ? He went to the

door and tried to open it ; it was locked.
An idea entered his mind : he was
in barracks somewhere ; the Military
Authorities must have got hold of him
somehow in spite of his exemption certificate. Or perhaps Pearl had gone and
enlisted. . . . He turned next to the
window, which was barred. Outside, he
could see a courtyard, filled, not with
soldiers, as he had expected, but a curious
motley crew of individuals, some men and
some women, wandering hither and thither
with an air of complete aimlessness.
Very odd, he thought—very odd. Beyond
the courtyard, on the farther side of a
phenomenally high wall, ran a railway line
and beyond it a village, roofed with tile
and thatch, and a tall church spire in the
midst. Dick looked carefully at the spire.
Didn't he know it ? Surely—yes, those
imbricated copper plates with which it
was covered, that gilded ship that served
as wind vane, the little gargoyles at the
corner of the tower—there could be no
doubt ; it was Belbury church. Belbury—that was where the . . . No, no ;
he wouldn't believe it. But looking down
again into that high-walled courtyard,

full of those queer, aimless folk, he was forced to admit it. The County Asylum stands at Belbury. He had often noticed it from the train, a huge, gaunt building of sausage-coloured brick, standing close to the railway, on the opposite side of the line to Belbury village and church. He remembered how, the last time he had passed in the train, he had wondered what they did in the asylum. He had regarded it then as one of those mysterious, un-approachable places, like Lhassa or a Ladies' Lavatory, into which he would never penetrate. And now, here he was, looking out through the bars, like any other madman. It was all Pearl's doing, as usual. If there had been no bars, he would have thrown himself out of the window.

He sat down on his bed and began to think about what he should do. He would have to be very sane and show them by his behaviour and speech that he was no more mad than the commonalty of mankind. He would be extremely dignified about it all. If a warder or a doctor or somebody came in to see him, he would rise to his feet and say in

the calmest and severest tones : " May I
ask, pray, why I am detained here and
upon whose authority ? " That ought
to stagger them. He practised that
sentence, and the noble attitude with
which he would accompany it, for the
best part of an hour. Then, suddenly,
there was the sound of a key in the lock.
He hastily sat down again on the bed.
A brisk little man of about forty, clean
shaven and with pince-nez, stepped into
the room, followed by a nurse and
a warder in uniform. The doctor !
Dick's heart was beating with absurd
violence ; he felt like an amateur actor
at the first performance of an imper-
fectly rehearsed play. He rose, rather
unsteadily, to his feet, and in a voice that
quavered a little with an emotion he
could not suppress, began :

" Pray I ask, may . . ."

Then, realizing that something had
gone wrong, he hesitated, stammered,
and came to a pause.

The doctor turned to the nurse.

" Did you hear that ? " he asked.   " He
called me May. He seems to think
everybody's a woman, not only himself."

8

Turning to Dick with a cheerful smile, he went on :

" Sit down, Miss Bellairs, please sit down."

It was too much. Dick burst into tears, flung himself upon the bed, and buried his face in the pillow. The doctor looked at him as he lay there sobbing, his whole body shaken and convulsed.

" A bad case, I fear."

And the nurse nodded.

For the next three days Dick refused to eat. It was certainly unreasonable, but it seemed the only way of making a protest. On the fourth day the doctor signed a certificate to the effect that forcible feeding had become necessary. Accompanied by two warders and a nurse, he entered Dick's room.

" Now, Miss Bellairs," he said, making a last persuasive appeal, " do have a little of this nice soup. We have come to have lunch with you."

" I refuse to eat," said Dick icily, " as a protest against my unlawful detention in this place. I am as sane as any of you here."

"Yes, yes." The doctor's voice was soothing. He made a sign to the warders. One was very large and stout, the other wiry, thin, sinister, like the second murderer in a play. They closed in on Dick.

"I won't eat and I won't be made to eat!" Dick cried. "Let me go!" he shouted at the fat warder, who had laid a hand on his shoulder. His temper was beginning to rise.

"Now, do behave yourself," said the fat warder. "It ain't a bit of use kicking up a row. Now, do take a little of this lovely soup," he added wheedlingly.

"Let me go!" Dick screamed again, all his self-control gone. "I will not let myself be bullied."

He began to struggle violently. The fat warder put an arm round his shoulders, as though he were an immense mother comforting an irritable child. Dick felt himself helpless; the struggle had quite exhausted him; he was weaker than he had any idea of. He began kicking the fat man's shins; it was the only way he could still show fight.

"Temper, temper," remonstrated the

warder, more motherly than ever. The thin warder stooped down, slipped a strap round the kicking legs, and drew it tight. Dick could move no more. His fury found vent in words—vain, abusive, filthy words, such as he had not used since he was a schoolboy.

" Let me go," he screamed—" let me go, you devils! You beasts, you swine! beasts and swine!" he howled again and again.

They soon had him securely strapped in a chair, his head held back ready for the doctor and his horrible-looking tubes. They were pushing the horrors up his nostrils. He coughed and choked, spat, shouted inarticulately, retched. It was like having a spoon put on your tongue and being told to say A-a-h, but worse; it was like jumping into the river and getting water up your nose—how he had always hated that!—only much worse. It was like almost everything unpleasant, only much, much worse than all. He exhausted himself struggling against his utterly immovable bonds. They had to carry him to his bed, he was so weak.

He lay there, unmoving—for he was unable to move—staring at the ceiling. He felt as though he were floating on air, unsupported, solid no longer; the sensation was not unpleasant. For that reason he refused to let his mind dwell upon it; he would think of nothing that was not painful, odious, horrible. He thought about the torture which had just been inflicted on him and of the monstrous injustice of which he was a victim. He thought of the millions who had been and were still being slaughtered in the war; he thought of their pain, all the countless separate pains of them; pain incommunicable, individual, beyond the reach of sympathy; infinities of pain pent within frail finite bodies; pain without sense or object, bringing with it no hope and no redemption, futile, unnecessary, stupid. In one supreme apocalyptic moment he saw, he felt the universe in all its horror.

They forcibly fed him again the following morning and again on the day after. On the fourth day pneumonia, the result of shock, complicated by acute inflammation of the throat and pleura, set in. The fever and pain gained ground. Dick had not the strength to resist their ravages, and his condition grew hourly worse. His mind, however, continued to work clearly—too clearly. It occurred to him that he might very likely die. He asked for pencil and paper to be brought him, and putting forth all the little strength he had left, he began to make his testament.

" I am perfectly sane," he wrote at the top of the page, and underlined the words three times. " I am confined here by the most intol. injust." As soon as he began, he realized how little time and strength were left him ; it was a waste to finish the long words. " They are killing me for my opins. I regard this war and all wars as utter bad. Capitalists' war. The devils will be smashed sooner later. Wish I could help. But it won't make any difference," he added on a new line and as though by an afterthought. " World will always be hell. Cap. or Lab., Engl. or Germ.— all beasts. One in a mill. is Good.

I wasn't. Selfish intellect. Perhaps Pearl Bellairs better. If die, send corp. to hosp. for anatomy. Useful for once in my life ! "

Quite suddenly, he lapsed into delirium. The clear lucidity of his mind became troubled. The real world disappeared from before his eyes, and in its place he saw a succession of bright, unsteady visions created by his sick fantasy. Scenes from his childhood, long forgotten, bubbled up and disappeared. Unknown, hideous faces crowded in upon him ; old friends revisited him. He was living in a bewildering mixture of the familiar and the strange. And all the while, across this changing unsubstantial world, there hurried a continual, interminable procession of dromedaries—countless high-domed beasts, with gargoyle faces and stiff legs and necks that bobbed as though on springs. Do what he could, he was unable to drive them away. He lost his temper with the brutes at last, struck at them, shouted ; but in vain. The room rang with his cries of, " Get away, you beasts. Bloody humps. None of your nonconformist faces here." And while he was yelling and gesticulating (with his left hand only), his right hand was still busily engaged in writing. The words were clear and legible ; the sentences consecutive and eminently sane. Dick might rave, but Pearl Bellairs remained calm and in full possession of her deplorable faculties. And what was Pearl doing with her busy pencil, while Dick, like a frenzied Betsy Trotwood, shouted at the trespassing camels ? The first thing she did was to scratch out all that poor Dick had said about the war. Underneath it she wrote :

" We shall not sheathe the sword, which we have not lightly . . ." And then, evidently finding that memorable sentence too long, particularly so since the addition of Poland and Czecho-Slovakia to the list of Allies, she began again.

" We are fighting for honour and the defence of Small Nationalities. Plucky little Belgium ! We went into the war with clean hands."

A little of Pearl's thought seemed at this moment to have slopped over into Dick's mind ; for he suddenly stopped abusing his dromedaries and began to cry out in the most pitiable fashion, " Clean hands, clean hands ! I can't get mine clean. I can't, I can't, I can't. I contaminate everything." And he kept rubbing his left hand against the bed-clothes and putting his fingers to his nose, only to exclaim, " Ugh, they still stink of goat ! " and then to start rubbing again.

The right hand wrote on unperturbed. " No peace with the Hun until he is crushed and humiliated. Self-respecting Britons will refuse to shake a Hunnish hand for many a long year after the war. No more German waiters. Intern the Forty-Seven Thousand Hidden Hands in High Places ! "

At this point, Pearl seemed to have been struck by a new idea. She took a clean page and began :

" To the Girls of England. I am a woman and proud of the fact. But, girls, I blushed for my sex to-day when I read in the papers that there had been cases of English girls talking to Hun prisoners, and not only talking to them, but allowing themselves to be kissed by them. Imagine ! Clean, healthy British girls allowing them-selves to be kissed by the swinish and bloodstained lips of the unspeakable Hun! Do you wonder that I blush for my sex? Stands England where she did? No, emphatically no, if these stories are true, and true—sadly and with a heavy bleeding heart do I admit it—true they are."

"Clean hands, clean hands," Dick was still muttering, and applying his fingers to his nose once more, "Christ," he cried, "how they stink! Goats, dung . . ."

"Is there any excuse for such conduct?" the pencil continued. "The most that can be said in palliation of the offence is that girls are thoughtless, that they do not consider the full significance of their actions. But listen to me, girls of all ages, classes and creeds, from the blue-eyed, light-hearted flapper of sixteen to the stern-faced, hard-headed business woman —listen to me. There is a girlish charm about thoughtlessness, but there is a point beyond which thoughtlessness becomes criminal. A flapper may kiss a Hun without thinking what she is doing, merely for the fun of the thing; perhaps, even, out of misguided pity. Will she repeat the offence if she realizes, as she must realize if she will only think, that this thoughtless fun, this mawkish and hysterical pity, is nothing less than Treason ? Treason—it is a sinister word, but . . ."

The pencil stopped writing ; even Pearl was beginning to grow tired. Dick's shouting had died away to a hoarse, faint whisper. Suddenly her attention was caught by the last words that Dick had written—the injunction to send his body, if he died, to a hospital for an anatomy. She put forth a great effort.

" NO. NO," she wrote in huge capitals. " Bury me in a little country churchyard, with lovely marble angels like the ones in St. George's at Windsor, over Princess Charlotte's tomb. Not anatomy. Too horrible, too disgus . . ."

The coma which had blotted out Dick's mind fell now upon hers as well. Two hours later Dick Greenow was dead ; the fingers of his right hand still grasped a pencil. The scribbled papers were thrown away as being merely the written ravings of a madman ; they were accustomed to that sort of thing at the asylum.

HAPPILY EVER AFTER

I

AT the best of times it is a long way
from Chicago to Blaybury in
Wiltshire, but war has fixed between
them a great gulf. In the circumstances,
therefore, it seemed an act of singular
devotion on the part of Peter Jacobsen
to have come all the way from the
Middle West, in the fourth year of war,
on a visit to his old friend Petherton,
when the project entailed a single-
handed struggle with two Great Powers
over the question of passports and the
risk, when they had been obtained, of
perishing miserably by the way, a victim
of frightfulness.

At the expense of much time and
more trouble Jacobsen had at last arrived ;
the gulf between Chicago and Blaybury
was spanned. In the hall of Petherton's
house a scene of welcome was being
enacted under the dim gaze of six or seven

brown family portraits by unknown
masters of the eighteenth and nineteenth
centuries.

Old Alfred Petherton, a grey shawl
over his shoulders—for he had to be
careful, even in June, of draughts and
colds—was shaking his guest's hand with
interminable cordiality.

" My dear boy," he kept repeating,
" it *is* a pleasure to see you. My dear
boy . . ."

Jacobsen limply abandoned his fore-
arm and waited in patience.

" I can never be grateful enough,"
Mr. Petherton went on—" never grateful
enough to you for having taken all this
endless trouble to come and see an old
decrepit man—for that's what I am now,
that's what I am, believe me."

" Oh, I assure you . . . " said Jacobsen,
with vague deprecation. " Le vieux
crétin qui pleurniche," he said to himself. French was a wonderfully expres-
sive language, to be sure.

" My digestion and my heart have got
much worse since I saw you last. But I
think I must have told you about that
in my letters."

" You did indeed, and I was most grieved to hear it."

" Grieved "—what a curious flavour that word had ! Like somebody's tea which used to recall the most delicious blends of forty years ago. But it was decidedly the *mot juste*. It had the right obituary note about it.

" Yes," Mr. Petherton continued, " my palpitations are very bad now. Aren't they, Marjorie ? " He appealed to his daughter who was standing beside him.

" Father's palpitations are very bad," she replied dutifully.

It was as though they were talking about some precious heirloom long and lovingly cherished.

" And my digestion. . . . This physical infirmity makes all mental activity so difficult. All the same, I manage to do a little useful work. We'll discuss that later, though. You must be feeling tired and dusty after your journey down. I'll guide you to your room. Marjorie, will you get someone to take up his luggage ? "

" I can take it myself," said Jacobsen, and he picked up a small gladstone-bag that had been deposited by the door.

" Is that all ? " Mr. Petherton asked.

" Yes, that's all."

As one living the life of reason, Jacobsen objected to owning things. One so easily became the slave of things and not their master. He liked to be free ; he checked his possessive instincts and limited his possessions to the strictly essential. He was as much or as little at home at Blaybury or Pekin. He could have explained all this if he liked. But in the present case it wasn't worth taking the trouble.

" This is your humble chamber," said Mr. Petherton, throwing open the door of what was, indeed, a very handsome spare-room, bright with chintzes and cut flowers and silver candlesticks. " A poor thing, but your own."

Courtly grace ! Dear old man ! Apt quotation ! Jacobsen unpacked his bag and arranged its contents neatly and methodically in the various drawers and shelves of the wardrobe.

It was a good many years now since Jacobsen had come in the course of his grand educational tour to Oxford. He spent a couple of years there, for he liked the place, and its inhabitants were a source of unfailing amusement to him.

A Norwegian, born in the Argentine, educated in the United States, in France, and in Germany; a man with no nationality and no prejudices, enormously old in experience, he found something very new and fresh and entertaining about his fellow-students with their comic public-school traditions and fabulous ignorance of the world. He had quietly watched them doing their little antics, feeling all the time that a row of bars separated them from himself, and that he ought, after each particularly amusing trick, to offer them a bun or a handful of pea-nuts. In the intervals of sight-seeing in this strange and delightful Jardin des Plantes he read Greats, and it was through Aristotle that he had come into contact with Alfred Petherton, fellow and tutor of his college.

The name of Petherton is a respectable one in the academic world. You will find it on the title-page of such meritorious, if not exactly brilliant, books as

Plato's Predecessors, Three Scottish Meta-physicians, Introduction to the Study of Ethics, Essays in Neo-Idealism. Some of his works are published in cheap editions as text-books.

One of those curious inexplicable friendships that often link the most un-likely people had sprung up between tutor and pupil, and had lasted un-broken for upwards of twenty years. Petherton felt a fatherly affection for the younger man, together with a father's pride, now that Jacobsen was a man of world-wide reputation, in having, as he supposed, spiritually be-gotten him. And now Jacobsen had travelled three or four thousand miles across a world at war just to see the old man. Petherton was profoundly touched.

" Did you see any submarines on the way over ? " Marjorie asked, as she and Jacobsen were strolling together in the garden after breakfast the next day.

" I didn't notice any ; but then I am very unobservant about these things."

There was a pause. At last, " I sup-

9

pose there is a great deal of war-work being done in America now?" said Marjorie.

Jacobsen supposed so; and there floated across his mind a vision of massed bands, of orators with megaphones, of patriotic sky-signs, of streets made perilous by the organized highway robbery of Red Cross collectors. He was too lazy to describe it all; besides, she wouldn't see the point of it.

"I should like to be able to do some war-work," Marjorie explained apologetically. "But I have to look after father, and there's the housekeeping, so I really haven't the time."

Jacobsen thought he detected a formula for the benefit of strangers. She evidently wanted to make things right about herself in people's minds. Her remark about the housekeeping made Jacobsen think of the late Mrs. Petherton, her mother; she had been a good-looking, painfully sprightly woman with a hankering to shine in University society at Oxford. One quickly learned that she was related to bishops and country families; a hunter of ecclesiastical lions and a snob.   He felt glad she was dead.

"Won't it be awful when there's no war-work," he said.   "People will have nothing to do or think about when peace comes."

"I shall be glad.   Housekeeping will be so much easier."

"True.   There are consolations."

Marjorie looked at him suspiciously ; she didn't like being laughed at.   What an undistinguished-looking little man he was !   Short, stoutish, with waxed brown moustaches and a forehead that incipient baldness had made interminably high.   He looked like the sort of man to whom one says : "Thank you, I'll take it in notes with a pound's worth of silver."   There were pouches under his eyes and pouches under his chin, and you could never guess from his expression what he was thinking about.   She was glad that she was taller than he and could look down on him.

Mr. Petherton appeared from the house, his grey shawl over his shoulders and the crackling expanse of the *Times* between his hands.

" Good morrow," he cried.

To the Shakespearian heartiness of this greeting Marjorie returned her most icily modern " Morning." Her father always said " Good morrow " instead of " Good morning," and the fact irritated her with unfailing regularity every day of her life.

" There's a most interesting account," said Mr. Petherton, " by a young pilot of an air fight in to-day's paper," and as they walked up and down the gravel path he read the article, which was a column and a half in length.

Marjorie made no attempt to disguise her boredom, and occupied herself by reading something on the other side of the page, craning her neck round to see.

" Very interesting," said Jacobsen when it was finished.

Mr. Petherton had turned over and was now looking at the Court Circular page.

" I see," he said, " there's someone called Beryl Camberley-Belcher going to be married. Do you know if that's any relation of the Howard Camberley-Belchers, Marjorie ? "

" I've no idea who the Howard Camberley-Belchers are," Marjorie answered rather sharply.

"Oh, I thought you did. Let me see. Howard Camberley-Belcher was at college with me. And he had a brother called James—or was it William?—and a sister who married one of the Riders, or at any rate some relation of the Riders; for I know the Camberley-Belchers and the Riders used to fit in somewhere. Dear me, I'm afraid my memory for names is going."

Marjorie went indoors to prepare the day's domestic campaign with the cook. When that was over she retired to her sitting-room and unlocked her very private desk. She must write to Guy this morning. Marjorie had known Guy Lambourne for years and years, almost as long as she could remember. The Lambournes were old family friends of the Pethertons : indeed they were, distantly, connections; they "fitted in somewhere," as Mr. Petherton would say—somewhere, about a couple of generations back. Marjorie was two years younger than Guy; they were both only children; circumstances had naturally thrown them a great deal together. Then Guy's father had died, and not long afterwards his mother, and at the age of seventeen Guy had actually come to live with the Pethertons, for the old man was his guardian. And now they were engaged; had been, more or less, from the first year of the war.

Marjorie took pen, ink, and paper. "DEAR GUY," she began—(" *We* aren't sentimental," she had once remarked, with a mixture of contempt and secret envy, to a friend who had confided that she and her fiancé never began with anything less than Darling.)—"I am longing for another of your letters. . . ." She went through the usual litany of longing. "It was father's birthday yesterday; he is sixty-five. I cannot bear to think that some day you and I will be as old as that. Aunt Ellen sent him a Stilton cheese—a useful war-time present. How boring housekeeping is. By dint of thinking about cheeses my mind is rapidly turning into one—a Gruyère; where there isn't cheese there are just holes, full of vacuum . . . "

She didn't really mind housekeeping so

much. She took it for granted, and did it just because it was there to be done. Guy, on the contrary, never took anything for granted ; she made these demonstrations for his benefit.

" I read Keats's letters, as you suggested, and thought them *too* beautiful . . ."

At the end of a page of rapture she paused and bit her pen. What was there to say next ? It seemed absurd one should have to write letters about the books one had been reading. But there was nothing else to write about ; nothing ever happened. After all, what had happened in her life ? Her mother dying when she was sixteen ; then the excitement of Guy coming to live with them ; then the war, but that hadn't meant much to her ; then Guy falling in love, and their getting engaged. That was really all. She wished she could write about her feelings in an accurate, complicated way, like people in novels ; but when she came to think about it, she didn't seem to have any feelings to describe.

She looked at Guy's last letter from France. " Sometimes," he had written, " I am tortured by an intense physical desire for you. I can think of nothing but your beauty, your young, strong body. I hate that ; I have to struggle to repress it. Do you forgive me ? " It rather thrilled her that he should feel like that about her : he had always been so cold, so reserved, so much opposed to sentimentality—to the kisses and endearments she would, perhaps, secretly have liked. But he had seemed so right when he said, " We must love like rational beings, with our minds, not with our hands and lips." All the same . . .

She dipped her pen in the ink and began to write again. " I know the feelings you spoke of in your letter. Sometimes I long for you in the same way. I dreamt the other night I was holding you in my arms, and woke up hugging the pillow." She looked at what she had written. It was too awful, too vulgar ! She would have to scratch it out. But no, she would leave it in spite of everything, just to see what he would think about it. She finished the letter quickly, sealed and stamped it, and rang for the maid to take it to the post. When the servant had gone, she shut up her desk with a bang. Bang—the letter had gone, irrevocably.

She picked up a large book lying on the table and began to read. It was the first volume of the *Decline and Fall*. Guy had said she must read Gibbon; she wouldn't be educated till she had read Gibbon. And so yesterday she had gone to her father in his library to get the book.

"Gibbon," Mr. Petherton had said, "certainly, my dear. How delightful it is to look at these grand old books again. One always finds something new every time."

Marjorie gave him to understand that she had never read it. She felt rather proud of her ignorance.

Mr. Petherton handed the first of eleven volumes to her. "A great book," he murmured—"an essential book. It fills the gap between your classical history and your mediæval stuff."

"Your" classical history, Marjorie repeated to herself, "your" classical history indeed! Her father had an irritating way of taking it for granted that she knew everything, that classical history was as much hers as his. Only a day or two before he had turned to her at luncheon with, "Do you remember, dear child, whether it was Pomponazzi who denied the personal immortality of the soul, or else that queer fellow, Laurentius Valla ? It's gone out of my head for the moment." Marjorie had quite lost her temper at the question—much to the innocent bewilderment of her poor father.

She had set to work with energy on the Gibbon ; her bookmarker registered the fact that she had got through one hundred and twenty-three pages yesterday. Marjorie started reading. After two pages she stopped. She looked at the number of pages still remaining to be read—and this was only the first volume. She felt like a wasp sitting down to eat a vegetable marrow. Gibbon's bulk was not perceptibly diminished by her first bite. It was too long. She shut the book and went out for a walk. Passing the Whites' house, she saw her friend, Beatrice White that was, sitting on the lawn with her two babies. Beatrice hailed her, and she turned in.

" Pat a cake, pat a cake," she said. At the age of ten months, baby John had already learnt the art of patting cakes. He slapped the outstretched hand offered

him, and his face, round and smooth and
pink like an enormous peach, beamed with
pleasure.

" Isn't he a darling ! " Marjorie
exclaimed. " You know, I'm sure he's
grown since last I saw him, which was on
Tuesday."

" He put on eleven ounces last week,"
Beatrice affirmed.

" How wonderful ! His hair's coming
on splendidly . . ."

It was Sunday the next day. Jacobsen
appeared at breakfast in the neatest of
black suits. He looked, Marjorie thought,
more than ever like a cashier. She longed
to tell him to hurry up or he'd miss the
8.53 for the second time this week and
the manager would be annoyed. Marjorie
herself was, rather consciously, not in
Sunday best.

" What is the name of the Vicar ? "
Jacobsen inquired, as he helped himself
to bacon.

" Trubshaw. Luke Trubshaw, I
believe."

" Does he preach well ? "

" He didn't when I used to hear him.

But I don't often go to church now, so
I don't know what he's like these
days."

"Why don't you go to church?"
Jacobsen inquired, with a silkiness of tone
which veiled the crude outlines of his
leading question.

Marjorie was painfully conscious of
blushing. She was filled with rage
against Jacobsen. "Because," she said
firmly, "I don't think it necessary to
give expression to my religious feelings
by making a lot of"—she hesitated
a moment—"a lot of meaningless gestures
with a crowd of other people."

"You used to go," said Jacobsen.

"When I was a child and hadn't
thought about these things."

Jacobsen was silent, and concealed a
smile in his coffee-cup. Really, he said
to himself, there ought to be religious
conscription for women—and for most
men, too. It was grotesque the way
these people thought they could stand by
themselves—the fools, when there was
the infinite authority of organized religion
to support their ridiculous feebleness.

"Does Lambourne go to church?"

he asked maliciously, and with an air of
perfect naïveté and good faith.

Marjorie coloured again, and a fresh
wave of hatred surged up within her.
Even as she had said the words she had
wondered whether Jacobsen would notice
that the phrase "meaningless gestures"
didn't ring very much like one of her
own coinages. "Gesture"—that was
one of Guy's words, like "incredible,"
"exacerbate," "impinge," "sinister." Of
course all her present views about religion
had come from Guy. She looked Jacobsen
straight in the face and replied :

"Yes, I think he goes to church
pretty regularly. But I really don't know :
his religion has nothing to do with me."

Jacobsen was lost in delight and
admiration.

Punctually at twenty minutes to eleven
he set out for church. From where she
was sitting in the summer-house Marjorie
watched him as he crossed the garden,
incredibly absurd and incongruous in his
black clothes among the blazing flowers
and the young emerald of the trees. Now
he was hidden behind the sweet-briar
hedge, all except the hard black melon of

his bowler hat, which she could see bobbing along between the topmost sprays.

She went on with her letter to Guy. ". . . What a strange man Mr. Jacobsen is. I suppose he is very clever, but I can't get very much out of him. We had an argument about religion at breakfast this morning; I rather scored off him. He has now gone off to church all by himself;—I really couldn't face the prospect of going with him—I hope he'll enjoy old Mr. Trubshaw's preaching!"

Jacobsen did enjoy Mr. Trubshaw's preaching enormously. He always made a point, in whatever part of Christendom he happened to be, of attending divine service. He had the greatest admiration of churches as institutions. In their solidity and unchangeableness he saw one of the few hopes for humanity. Further, he derived great pleasure from comparing the Church as an institution—splendid, powerful, eternal — with the childish imbecility of its representatives. How delightful it was to sit in the herded congregation and listen to the sincere outpourings of an intellect only a little less limited than that of an Australian

aboriginal ! How restful to feel oneself
a member of a flock, guided by a good
shepherd—himself a sheep ! Then there
was the scientific interest (he went to
church as student of anthropology, as a
Freudian psychologist) and the philosophic amusement of counting the un-
distributed middles and tabulating
historically the exploded fallacies in the
parson's discourse.

To-day Mr. Trubshaw preached a
topical sermon about the Irish situation.
His was the gospel of the *Morning Post*,
slightly tempered by Christianity. It
was our duty, he said, to pray for the Irish
first of all, and if that had no effect upon
recruiting, why, then, we must conscribe
them as zealously as we had prayed before.

Jacobsen leaned back in his pew with a
sigh of contentment. A connoisseur, he
recognized that this was the right stuff.

"Well," said Mr. Petherton over the
Sunday beef at lunch, "how did you like
our dear Vicar ? "

"He was splendid," said Jacobsen, with
grave enthusiasm. "One of the best
sermons I've ever heard."

"Indeed ? I shall really have to go and

hear him again. It must be nearly ten years since I listened to him."

" He's inimitable."

Marjorie looked at Jacobsen carefully. He seemed to be perfectly serious. She was more than ever puzzled by the man.

The days went slipping by, hot blue days that passed like a flash almost without one's noticing them, cold grey days, seeming interminable and without number, and about which one spoke with a sense of justified grievance, for the season was supposed to be summer. There was fighting going on in France — terrific battles, to judge from the headlines in the *Times* ; but, after all, one day's paper was very much like another's. Marjorie read them dutifully, but didn't honestly take in very much ; at least she forgot about things very soon. She couldn't keep count with the battles of Ypres, and when somebody told her that she ought to go and see the photographs of the *Vindictive*, she smiled vaguely and said Yes, without remembering precisely what the *Vindictive* was—a ship, she supposed.

Guy was in France, to be sure, but he was an Intelligence Officer now, so that she was hardly anxious about him at all. Clergymen used to say that the war was bringing us all back to a sense of the fundamental realities of life. She supposed it was true : Guy's enforced absences were a pain to her, and the difficulties of housekeeping continually increased and multiplied.

Mr. Petherton took a more intelligent interest in the war than did his daughter. He prided himself on being able to see the thing as a whole, on taking an historical, God's-eye view of it all. He talked about it at meal-times, insisting that the world must be made safe for democracy. Between meals he sat in the library working at his monumental History of Morals. To his dinner-table disquisitions Marjorie would listen more or less attentively, Jacobsen with an unfailing, bright, intelligent politeness. Jacobsen himself rarely volunteered a remark about the war ; it was taken for granted that he thought about it in the same way as all other right-thinking folk. Between meals he worked in his room or discussed the morals of the Italian Renaissance with his host. Marjorie

10

could write to Guy that nothing was happening, and that but for his absence and the weather interfering so much with tennis, she would be perfectly happy.

Into the midst of this placidity there fell, delightful bolt from the blue, the announcement that Guy was getting leave at the end of July. "DARLING," Marjorie wrote, "I am so excited to think that you will be with me in such a little—such a long, long time." Indeed, she was so excited and delighted that she realized with a touch of remorse how comparatively little she had thought of him when there seemed no chance of seeing him, how dim a figure in absence he was. A week later she heard that George White had arranged to get leave at the same time so as to see Guy. She was glad; George was a charming boy, and Guy was so fond of him. The Whites were their nearest neighbours, and ever since Guy had come to live at Blaybury he had seen a great deal of young George.

"We shall be a most festive party," said Mr. Petherton. "Roger will be coming to us just at the same time as Guy."

" I'd quite forgotten Uncle Roger," said Marjorie. " Of course, his holidays begin then, don't they ? "

The Reverend Roger was Alfred Petherton's brother and a master at one of our most glorious public schools. Marjorie hardly agreed with her father in thinking that his presence would add anything to the " festiveness " of the party. It was a pity he should be coming at this particular moment. However, we all have our little cross to bear.

Mr. Petherton was feeling playful. " We must bring down," he said, " the choicest Falernian, bottled when Gladstone was consul, for the occasion. We must prepare wreaths and unguents and hire a flute player and a couple of dancing girls . . ."

He spent the rest of the meal in quoting Horace, Catullus, the Greek Anthology, Petronius, and Sidonius Apollinarius. Marjorie's knowledge of the dead languages was decidedly limited. Her thoughts were elsewhere, and it was only dimly and as it were through a mist that she heard her father murmuring— whether merely to himself or with the

hope of eliciting an answer from somebody, she hardly knew—" Let me see :
how does that epigram go ?—that one
about the different kinds of fish and
the garlands of roses, by Meleager, or is
it Poseidippus ? . . ."

II

GUY and Jacobsen were walking
in the Dutch garden, an incongruous couple. On Guy military
servitude had left no outwardly visible
mark ; out of uniform, he still looked
like a tall, untidy undergraduate ; he
stooped and drooped as much as ever ;
his hair was still bushy and, to judge by
the dim expression of his face, he had not
yet learnt to think imperially. His khaki
always looked like a disguise, like the
most absurd fancy dress. Jacobsen trotted
beside him, short, fattish, very sleek, and
correct. They talked in a desultory way
about things indifferent. Guy, anxious
for a little intellectual exercise after so
many months of discipline, had been
trying to inveigle his companion into
a philosophical discussion. Jacobsen con-

sistently eluded his efforts ; he was too
lazy to talk seriously ; there was no
profit that he could see to be got out of
this young man's opinions, and he had
not the faintest desire to make a dis-
ciple. He preferred, therefore, to discuss the war and the weather. It irritated him that people should want to
trespass on the domain of thought—
people who had no right to live anywhere but on the vegetative plane of
mere existence. He wished they would
simply be content to *be* or *do*, not try,
so hopelessly, to think, when only one in
a million can think with the least profit
to himself or anyone else.

Out of the corner of his eye he looked
at the dark, sensitive face of his companion ; he ought to have gone into
business at eighteen, was Jacobsen's
verdict. It was bad for him to think ;
he wasn't strong enough.

A great sound of barking broke upon
the calm of the garden. Looking up,
the two strollers saw George White
running across the green turf of the
croquet lawn with a huge fawn-coloured
dog bounding along at his side.

"Morning," he shouted. He was hatless and out of breath. "I was taking Bella for a run, and thought I'd look in and see how you all were."

"What a lovely dog!" Jacobsen exclaimed.

"An old English mastiff—our one aboriginal dog. She has a pedigree going straight back to Edward the Confessor."

Jacobsen began a lively conversation with George on the virtues and shortcomings of dogs. Bella smelt his calves and then lifted up her gentle black eyes to look at him. She seemed satisfied.

He looked at them for a little; they were too much absorbed in their doggy conversation to pay attention to him. He made a gesture as though he had suddenly remembered something, gave a little grunt, and with a very preoccupied expression on his face turned to go towards the house. His elaborate piece of by-play escaped the notice of the intended spectators; Guy saw that it had, and felt more miserable and angry and jealous than ever. They would think he had slunk off because he wasn't wanted—which was quite true—instead of believing that he had something very important to do, which was what he had intended they should believe.

A cloud of self-doubt settled upon him. Was his mind, after all, worthless, and the little things he had written—rubbish, not potential genius as he had hoped? Jacobsen was right in preferring George's company. George was perfect, physically, a splendid creature; what could he himself claim?

"I'm second-rate," he thought—"second-rate, physically, morally, mentally. Jacobsen is quite right."

The best he could hope to be was a pedestrian literary man with quiet tastes.

NO, no, no! He clenched his hands and, as though to register his resolve before the universe, he said, aloud:

"I will do it; I will be first-rate, I will."

He was covered with confusion on seeing a gardener pop up, surprised from behind a bank of rose-bushes. Talking to himself—the man must have thought him mad!

He hurried on across the lawn, entered the house, and ran upstairs to his room.

There was not a second to lose ; he must begin at once. He would write something—something that would last, solid, hard, shining. . . .

"Damn them all ! I will do it, I can . . ."

There were writing materials and a table in his room. He selected a pen— with a Relief nib he would be able to go on for hours without getting tired—and a large square sheet of writing-paper.

"HATCH HOUSE,
BLAYBURY,
WILTS.
Station : Cogham, 3 miles ; Nobes Monacorum, 4½ miles."

Stupid of people to have their stationery printed in red, when black or blue is so much nicer ! He inked over the letters.

He held up the paper to the light ; there was a watermark, "Pimlico Bond." What an admirable name for the hero of a novel ! Pimlico Bond. . . .

"There's be-eef in the la-arder
And du-ucks in the pond ;
Crying dilly dilly, dilly dilly . . ."

He bit the end of his pen. "What I want to get," he said to himself, "is something very hard, very external. Intense emotion, but one will somehow have got outside it." He made a movement of hands, arms, and shoulders, tightening his muscles in an effort to express to himself physically that hardness and tightness and firmness of style after which he was struggling.

He began to draw on his virgin paper. A woman, naked, one arm lifted over her head, so that it pulled up her breast by that wonderful curving muscle that comes down from the shoulder. The inner surface of the thighs, remember, is slightly concave. The feet, seen from the front, are always a difficulty.

It would never do to leave that about. What would the servants think? He turned the nipples into eyes, drew heavy lines for nose, mouth, and chin, slopped on the ink thick; it made a passable face now—though an acute observer might have detected the original nudity. He tore it up into very small pieces.

A crescendo booming filled the house. It was the gong. He looked at his watch.

Lunch-time, and he had done nothing.
O God! . . .

III

IT was dinner-time on the last evening of Guy's leave. The un-
covered mahogany table was like a pool
of brown unruffled water within whose
depths flowers and the glinting shapes of
glass and silver hung dimly reflected.
Mr. Petherton sat at the head of the
board, flanked by his brother Roger and
Jacobsen. Youth, in the persons of
Marjorie, Guy, and George White, had
collected at the other end. They had
reached the stage of dessert.

"This is excellent port," said Roger,
sleek and glossy like a well-fed black cob
under his silken clerical waistcoat. He
was a strong, thick-set man of about fifty,
with a red neck as thick as his head. His
hair was cropped with military closeness;
he liked to set a good example to the
boys, some of whom showed distressing
"æsthetic" tendencies and wore their
hair long.

"I'm glad you like it. I mayn't touch
it myself, of course. Have another

glass." Alfred Petherton's face wore an expression of dyspeptic melancholy. He was wishing he hadn't taken quite so much of that duck.

"Thank you, I will." Roger took the decanter with a smile of satisfaction. "The tired schoolmaster is worthy of his second glass. White, you look rather pale ; I think you must have another." Roger had a hearty, jocular manner, calculated to prove to his pupils that he was not one of the slimy sort of parsons, not a Creeping Jesus.

There was an absorbing conversation going on at the youthful end of the table. Secretly irritated at having been thus interrupted in the middle of it, White turned round and smiled vaguely at Roger.

"Oh, thank you, sir," he said, and pushed his glass forward to be filled. The " sir " slipped out unawares ; it was, after all, such a little while since he had been a schoolboy under Roger's dominion.

"One is lucky," Roger went on seriously, " to get any port wine at all now. I'm thankful to say I bought ten dozen

from my old college some years ago to
lay down ; otherwise I don't know what
I should do. My wine merchant tells
me he couldn't let me have a single
bottle. Indeed, he offered to buy some
off me, if I'd sell. But I wasn't having
any. A bottle in the cellar is worth ten
shillings in the pocket these days. I
always say that port has become a
necessity now one gets so little meat.
Lambourne ! you are another of our
brave defenders ; you deserve a second
glass."

" No, thanks," said Guy, hardly looking up. " I've had enough." He went
on talking to Marjorie — about the
different views of life held by the French
and the Russians.

Roger helped himself to cherries.
" One has to select them carefully," he
remarked for the benefit of the unwillingly
listening George. " There is nothing
that gives you such stomach - aches as
unripe cherries."

" I expect you're glad, Mr. Petherton,
that holidays have begun at last ? " said
Jacobsen.

" Glad ? I should think so. One is

utterly dead beat at the end of the summer term. Isn't one, White ? "

White had taken the opportunity to turn back again and listen to Guy's conversation ; recalled, like a dog who has started off on a forbidden scent, he obediently assented that one did get tired at the end of the summer term.

" I suppose," said Jacobsen, " you still teach the same old things—Cæsar, Latin verses, Greek grammar, and the rest ? We Americans can hardly believe that all that still goes on."

" Thank goodness," said Roger, " we still hammer a little solid stuff into them. But there's been a great deal of fuss lately about new curriculums and so forth. They do a lot of science now and things of that kind, but I don't believe the children learn anything at all. It's pure waste of time."

" So is all education, I dare say," said Jacobsen lightly.

" Not if you teach them discipline. That's what's wanted—discipline. Most of these little boys need plenty of beating, and they don't get enough now. Besides, if you can't hammer knowledge in at their heads, you can at least beat a little in at their tails."

"You're very ferocious, Roger," said Mr. Petherton, smiling. He was feeling better ; the duck was settling down.

"No, it's the vital thing. The best thing the war has brought us is discipline. The country had got slack and wanted tightening up." Roger's face glowed with zeal.

From the other end of the table Guy's voice could be heard saying, "Do you know César Franck's 'Dieu s'avance à travers la lande' ? It's one of the finest bits of religious music I know."

Mr. Petherton's face lighted up ; he leaned forward. "No," he said, throwing his answer unexpectedly into the midst of the young people's conversation. "I don't know it ; but do you know this ? Wait a minute." He knitted his brows, and his lips moved as though he were trying to recapture a formula. "Ah, I've got it. Now, can you tell me this ? The name of what famous piece of religious music do I utter when I order an old carpenter, once a Liberal but now a renegade to Conservatism, to make a hive for bees ? "

Guy gave it up ; his guardian beamed delightedly.

"Hoary Tory, oh, Judas ! Make a bee-house," he said. "Do you see ? Oratorio *Judas Maccabeus*."

Guy could have wished that this bit of flotsam from Mr. Petherton's sportive youth had not been thus washed up at his feet. He felt that he had been peeping indecently close into the dark backward and abysm of time.

"That was a good one," Mr. Petherton chuckled. "I must see if I can think of some more."

Roger, who was not easily to be turned away from his favourite topic, waited till this irrelevant spark of levity had quite expired, and continued : "It's a remarkable and noticeable fact that you never seem to get discipline combined with the teaching of science or modern languages. Who ever heard of a science master having a good house at a school ? Scientists' houses are always bad."

"How very strange ! " said Jacobsen.

"Strange, but a fact. It seems to me

a great mistake to give them houses at all if they can't keep discipline. And then there's the question of religion. Some of these men never come to chapel except when they're on duty. And then, I ask you, what happens when they prepare their boys for Confirmation ? Why, I've known boys come to me who were supposed to have been prepared by one or other of these men, and, on asking them, I've found that they know nothing whatever about the most solemn facts of the Eucharist.—May I have some more of those excellent cherries please, White ? —Of course, I do my best in such cases to tell the boys what I feel personally about these solemn things. But there generally isn't the time ; one's life is so crowded ; and so they go into Confirmation with only the very haziest knowledge of what it's all about. You see how absurd it is to let anyone but the classical men have anything to do with the boys' lives."

" Shake it well, dear," Mr. Petherton was saying to his daughter, who had come with his medicine.

" What is that stuff ? " asked Roger.

" Oh, it's merely my peptones. I can hardly digest at all without it, you know."

" You have all my sympathies. My poor colleague, Flexner, suffers from chronic colitis. I can't imagine how he goes on with his work."

" No, indeed. I find I can do nothing strenuous."

Roger turned and seized once more on the unhappy George. " White," he said, " let this be a lesson to you. Take care of your inside ; it's the secret of a happy old age."

Guy looked up quickly. " Don't worry about his old age," he said in a strange harsh voice, very different from the gentle, elaborately modulated tone in which he generally spoke. " He won't have an old age. His chances against surviving are about fourteen to three if the war goes on another year."

" Come," said Roger, " don't let's be pessimistic."

" But I'm not. I assure you, I'm giving you a most rosy view of George's chance of reaching old age."

It was felt that Guy's remarks had been

11

in poor taste. There was a silence ; eyes floated vaguely and uneasily, trying not to encounter one another. Roger cracked a nut loudly. When he had sufficiently relished the situation, Jacobsen changed the subject by remarking :

" That was a fine bit of work by our destroyers this morning, wasn't it ? "

" It did one good to read about it," said Mr. Petherton. " Quite the Nelson touch."

Roger raised his glass. " Nelson ! " he said, and emptied it at a gulp. " What a man ! I am trying to persuade the Headmaster to make Trafalgar Day a holiday. It is the best way of reminding boys of things of that sort."

" A curiously untypical Englishman to be a national hero, isn't he ? " said Jacobsen. " So emotional and lacking in Britannic phlegm."

The Reverend Roger looked grave. " There's one thing I've never been able to understand about Nelson, and that is, how a man who was so much the soul of honour and of patriotism could have been—er—immoral with Lady Hamilton.

I know people say that it was the custom of the age, that these things meant nothing then, and so forth; but all the same, I repeat, I cannot understand how a man who was so intensely a patriotic Englishman could have done such a thing."

" I fail to see what patriotism has got to do with it," said Guy.

Roger fixed him with his most pedagogic look and said slowly and gravely, "Then I am sorry for you. I shouldn't have thought it was necessary to tell an Englishman that purity of morals is a national tradition: you especially, a public-school man."

" Let us go and have a hundred up at billiards," said Mr. Petherton. "Roger, will you come? And you, George, and Guy?"

" I'm so incredibly bad," Guy insisted, " I'd really rather not."

" So am I," said Jacobsen.

" Then, Marjorie, you must make the fourth."

The billiard players trooped out; Guy and Jacobsen were left alone, brooding over the wreckage of dinner. There was

a long silence. The two men sat smoking, Guy sitting in a sagging, crumpled
attitude, like a half-empty sack abandoned
on a chair, Jacobsen very upright and
serene.

"Do you find you can suffer fools
gladly?" asked Guy abruptly.

"Perfectly gladly."

"I wish I could. The Reverend Roger
has a tendency to make my blood boil."

"But such a good soul," Jacobsen
insisted.

"I dare say, but a monster all the same."

"You should take him more calmly. I
make a point of never letting myself be
moved by external things. I stick to my
writing and thinking. Truth is beauty,
beauty is truth, and so forth : after all,
they're the only things of solid value."
Jacobsen looked at the young man with a
smile as he said these words. There is no
doubt, he said to himself, that that boy
ought to have gone into business ; what a
mistake this higher education is, to be
sure.

"Of course, they're the only things,"
Guy burst out passionately. "You can
afford to say so because you had the luck

to be born twenty years before I was, and with five thousand miles of good deep water between you and Europe. Here am I, called upon to devote my life, in a very different way from which you devote yours to truth and beauty—to devote my life to—well, what ? I'm not quite sure, but I preserve a touching faith that it is good. And you tell me to ignore external circumstances. Come and live in Flanders a little and try . . ." He launched forth into a tirade about agony and death and blood and putrefaction.

"What is one to do ? " he concluded despairingly. "What the devil is right ? I had meant to spend my life writing and thinking, trying to create something beautiful or discover something true. But oughtn't one, after all, if one survives, to give up everything else and try to make this hideous den of a world a little more habitable ? "

" I think you can take it that a world which has let itself be dragooned into this criminal folly is pretty hopeless. Follow your inclinations ; or, better, go into a bank and make a lot of money."

Guy burst out laughing, rather too

loudly. "Admirable, admirable!" he said. "To return to our old topic of fools: frankly, Jacobsen, I cannot imagine why you should elect to pass your time with my dear old guardian. He's a charming old man, but one must admit——" He waved his hand.

"One must live somewhere," said Jacobsen. "I find your guardian a most interesting man to be with. — Oh, do look at that dog!" On the hearth-rug Marjorie's little Pekingese, Confucius, was preparing to lie down and go to sleep. He went assiduously through the solemn farce of scratching the floor, under the impression, no doubt, that he was making a comfortable nest to lie in. He turned round and round, scratching earnestly and methodically. Then he lay down, curled himself up in a ball, and was asleep in the twinkling of an eye.

"Isn't that too wonderfully human!" exclaimed Jacobsen delightedly. Guy thought he could see now why Jacobsen enjoyed living with Mr. Petherton. The old man was so wonderfully human.

Later in the evening, when the billiards

was over and Mr. Petherton had duly commented on the anachronism of introducing the game into Anthony and Cleopatra, Guy and Marjorie went for a stroll in the garden. The moon had risen above the trees and lit up the front of the house with its bright pale light that could not wake the sleeping colours of the world.

" Moonlight is the proper architectural light," said Guy, as they stood looking at the house. The white light and the hard black shadows brought out all the elegance of its Georgian symmetry.

" Look, here's the ghost of a rose." Marjorie touched a big cool flower, which one guessed rather than saw to be red, a faint equivocal lunar crimson. " And, oh, smell the tobacco-plant flowers. Aren't they delicious ! "

" I always think there's something very mysterious about perfume drifting through the dark like this. It seems to come from some perfectly different immaterial world, peopled by unembodied sensations, phantom passions. Think of the spiritual effect of incense in a dark church. One isn't surprised that people have believed in the existence of the soul."

They walked on in silence. Sometimes, accidentally, his hand would brush against hers in the movement of their march. Guy felt an intolerable emotion of expectancy, akin to fear. It made him feel almost physically sick.

" Do you remember," he said abruptly, " that summer holiday our families spent together in Wales ? It must have been nineteen four or five. I was ten and you were eight or thereabouts."

" Of course I remember," cried Marjorie. " Everything. There was that funny little toy railway from the slate quarries."

" And do you remember our gold-mine ? All those tons of yellow ironstone we collected and hoarded in a cave, fully believing they were nuggets. How incredibly remote it seems ! "

" And you had a wonderful process by which you tested whether the stuff was real gold or not. It all passed triumphantly as genuine, I remember ! "

" Having that secret together first made us friends, I believe."

" I dare say," said Marjorie. " Fourteen years ago—what a time ! And you began educating me even then : all that stuff you told me about gold-mining, for instance."

" Fourteen years," Guy repeated reflectively, " and I shall be going out again to-morrow . . ."

" Don't speak about it. I am so miserable when you're away." She genuinely forgot what a delightful summer she had had, except for the shortage of tennis.

" We must make this the happiest hour of our lives. Perhaps it may be the last we shall be together." Guy looked up at the moon, and he perceived, with a sudden start, that it was a sphere islanded in an endless night, not a flat disk stuck on a wall not so very far away. It filled him with an infinite dreariness ; he felt too insignificant to live at all.

" Guy, you mustn't talk like that," said Marjorie appealingly.

" We've got twelve hours," said Guy in a meditative voice, " but that's only clockwork time. You can give an hour the quality of everlastingness, and spend years which are as though they had never been. We get our immortality here and now ; it's a question of quality, not of quantity.

I don't look forward to golden harps or anything of that sort. I know that when I am dead, I shall be dead ; there isn't any afterwards. If I'm killed, my immortality will be in your memory. Perhaps, too, somebody will read the things I've written, and in his mind I shall survive, feebly and partially. But in your mind I shall survive intact and whole."

" But I'm sure we shall go on living after death. It can't be the end." Marjorie was conscious that she had heard those words before. Where ? Oh yes, it was earnest Evangeline who had spoken them at the school debating society.

"I wouldn't count on it," Guy replied, with a little laugh. " You may get such a disappointment when you die." Then in an altered voice, " I don't want to die. I hate and fear death. But probably I shan't be killed after all. All the same . . ." His voice faded out. They stepped into a tunnel of impenetrable darkness between two tall hornbeam hedges. He had become nothing but a voice, and now that had ceased ; he had disappeared. The voice began again, low, quick, monotonous, a little breathless. " I remember once reading a poem by one of the old Provençal troubadours, telling how God had once granted him supreme happiness ; for the night before he was to set out for the Crusade, it had been granted him to hold his lady in his arms— all the short eternal night through. Ains que j'aille oltre mer : when I was going beyond sea." The voice stopped again. They were standing at the very mouth of the hornbeam alley, looking out from that close-pent river of shadow upon an ocean of pale moonlight.

"How still it is." They did not speak ; they hardly breathed. They became saturated with the quiet.

Marjorie broke the silence. "Do you want me as much as all that, Guy ? " All through that long, speechless minute she had been trying to say the words, repeating them over to herself, longing to say them aloud, but paralysed, unable to. And at last she had spoken them, impersonally, as though through the mouth of someone else. She heard them very distinctly, and was amazed at the matter-of-factness of the tone.

Guy's answer took the form of a question.

" Well, suppose I were killed now,"
he said, " should I ever have really
lived ? "

They had stepped out of the cavernous
alley into the moonlight.   She could see
him clearly now, and there was something
so drooping and dejected and pathetic
about him, he seemed so much of a great,
overgrown child that a wave of passionate
pitifulness rushed through her, rein-
forcing other emotions less maternal.
She longed to take him in her arms, stroke
his hair, lullaby him, baby-fashion, to
sleep upon her breast.   And Guy, on his
side, desired nothing better than to
give his fatigues and sensibilities to her
maternal care, to have his eyes kissed fast,
and sleep to her soothing.   In his relations
with women—but his experience in this
direction was deplorably small—he had,
unconsciously at first but afterwards with
a realization of what he was doing, played
this child part.   In moments of self-
analysis he laughed at himself for acting
the " child stunt," as he called it.   Here
he was—he hadn't noticed it yet—doing
it again, drooping, dejected, wholly
pathetic, feeble . . .

Marjorie was carried away by her emotion. She would give herself to her lover, would take possession of her helpless, pitiable child. She put her arms round his neck, lifted her face to his kisses, whispered something tender and inaudible.

Guy drew her towards him and began kissing the soft, warm mouth. He touched the bare arm that encircled his neck; the flesh was resilient under his fingers; he felt a desire to pinch it and tear it.

It had been just like this with that little slut Minnie. Just the same —all horrible lust. He remembered a curious physiological fact out of Havelock Ellis. He shuddered as though he had touched something disgusting, and pushed her away.

" No, no, no. It's horrible; it's odious. Drunk with moonlight and sentiment-alizing about death. . . . Why not just say with Biblical frankness, Lie with me —Lie with me ? "

That this love, which was to have been so marvellous and new and beautiful, should end libidinously and bestially like the affair, never remembered without a shiver of shame, with Minnie (the vulgarity of her !)—filled him with horror.

Marjorie burst into tears and ran away, wounded and trembling, into the solitude of the hornbeam shadow. " Go away, go away," she sobbed, with such intensity of command that Guy, moved by an immediate remorse and the sight of tears to stop her and ask forgiveness, was constrained to let her go her ways.

A cool, impersonal calm had succeeded almost immediately to his outburst. Critically, he examined what he had done, and judged it, not without a certain feeling of satisfaction, to be the greatest " floater " of his life. But at least the thing was done and couldn't be undone. He took the weak-willed man's delight in the irrevocability of action. He walked up and down the lawn smoking a cigarette and thinking, clearly and quietly — remembering the past, questioning the future. When the cigarette was finished he went into the house.

He entered the smoking-room to hear Roger saying, ". . . It's the poor who are having the good time now. Plenty to eat, plenty of money, and no taxes to pay.

No taxes—that's the sickening thing. Look at Alfred's gardener, for instance. He gets twenty-five or thirty bob a week and an uncommon good house. He's married, but only has one child. A man like that is uncommonly well off. He ought to be paying income-tax ; he can perfectly well afford it."

Mr. Petherton was listening somnolently, Jacobsen with his usual keen, intelligent politeness ; George was playing with the blue Persian kitten.

It had been arranged that George should stay the night, because it was such a bore having to walk that mile and a bit home again in the dark. Guy took him up to his room and sat down on the bed for a final cigarette, while George was undressing. It was the hour of confidence— that rather perilous moment when fatigue has relaxed the fibres of the mind, making it ready and ripe for sentiment.

" It depresses me so much," said Guy, " to think that you're only twenty and that I'm just on twenty-four. You will be young and sprightly when the war ends ; I shall be an old antique man."

" Not so old as all that," George

answered, pulling off his shirt. His skin was very white, face, neck, and hands seeming dark brown by comparison; there was a sharply demarcated high-water mark of sunburn at throat and wrist.

"It horrifies me to think of the time one is wasting in this bloody war, growing stupider and grosser every day, achieving nothing at all. It will be five, six—God knows how many—years cut clean out of one's life. You'll have the world before you when it's all over, but I shall have spent my best time."

"Of course, it doesn't make so much difference to me," said George through a foam of tooth-brushing; "I'm not capable of doing anything of any particular value. It's really all the same whether I lead a blameless life broking stocks or spend my time getting killed. But for you, I agree, it's too bloody. . . ."

Guy smoked on in silence, his mind filled with a languid resentment against circumstance. George put on his pyjamas and crept under the sheet ; he had to curl himself up into a ball, because Guy was lying across the end of the bed, and he couldn't put his feet down.

" I suppose," said Guy at last, meditatively—" I suppose the only consolations are, after all, women and wine. I shall really have to resort to them. Only women are mostly so fearfully boring and wine is so expensive now."

" But not all women ! " George, it was evident, was waiting to get a confidence off his chest.

" I gather you've found the exceptions."

George poured forth. He had just spent six months at Chelsea—six dreary months on the barrack square ; but there had been lucid intervals between the drills and the special courses, which he had filled with many notable voyages of discovery among unknown worlds. And chiefly, Columbus to his own soul, he had discovered all those psychological intricacies and potentialities, which only the passions bring to light. *Nosce teipsum*, it has been commanded ; and a judicious cultivation of the passions is one of the surest roads to self-knowledge. To George, at barely twenty, it was all so amazingly new and exciting, and Guy listened to the story of his adventures

12

with admiration and a touch of envy. He regretted the dismal and cloistered chastity — broken only once, and how sordidly ! Wouldn't he have learnt much more, he wondered—have been a more real and better human being if he had had George's experiences ? He would have profited by them more than George could ever hope to do. There was the risk of George's getting involved in a mere foolish expense of spirit in a waste of shame. He might not be sufficiently an individual to remain himself in spite of his surroundings ; his hand would be coloured by the dye he worked in. Guy felt sure that he himself would have run no risk ; he would have come, seen, conquered, and returned intact and still himself, but enriched by the spoils of a new knowledge. Had he been wrong after all ? Had life in the cloister of his own philosophy been wholly unprofitable ?

He looked at George. It was not surprising that the ladies favoured him, glorious ephebus that he was.

" With a face and figure like mine," he reflected, " I shouldn't have been able

to lead his life, even if I'd wanted to."
He laughed inwardly.

" You really must meet her," George
was saying enthusiastically.

Guy smiled. " No, I really mustn't.
Let me give you a bit of perfectly good
advice. Never attempt to share your
joys with anyone else. People will
sympathize with pain, but not with
pleasure. Good night, George."

He bent over the pillow and kissed
the smiling face that was as smooth as a
child's to his lips.

Guy lay awake for a long time, and
his eyes were dry and aching before
sleep finally came upon him. He spent
those dark interminable hours thinking
—thinking hard, intensely, painfully.
No sooner had he left George's room than
a feeling of intense unhappiness took
hold of him. " Distorted with misery,"
that was how he described himself ; he
loved to coin such phrases, for he felt
the artist's need to express as well as to
feel and think. Distorted with misery,
he went to bed ; distorted with misery,
he lay and thought and thought. He
had, positively, a sense of physical

distortion : his guts were twisted, he had a hunched back, his legs were withered. . . .

He had the right to be miserable. He was going back to France to-morrow, he had trampled on his mistress's love, and he was beginning to doubt himself, to wonder whether his whole life hadn't been one ludicrous folly.

He reviewed his life, like a man about to die. Born in another age, he would, he supposed, have been religious. He had got over religion early, like the measles— at nine a Low Churchman, at twelve a Broad Churchman, and at fourteen an Agnostic—but he still retained the temperament of a religious man. Intellectually he was a Voltairian, emotionally a Bunyanite. To have arrived at this formula was, he felt, a distinct advance in self-knowledge. And what a fool he had been with Marjorie ! The priggishness of his attitude—making her read Wordsworth when she didn't want to. Intellectual love — his phrases weren't always a blessing ; how hopelessly he had deceived himself with words ! And now this evening the crowning outrage, when he had behaved to her like a hysterical anchorite dealing with a temptation. His body tingled, at the recollection, with shame.

An idea occurred to him ; he would go and see her, tiptoe downstairs to her room, kneel by her bed, ask for her forgiveness. He lay quite still imagining the whole scene. He even went so far as to get out of bed, open the door, which made a noise in the process like a peacock's scream, quite unnerving him, and creep to the head of the stairs. He stood there a long time, his feet growing colder and colder, and then decided that the adventure was really too sordidly like the episode at the beginning of Tolstoy's *Resurrection*. The door screamed again as he returned ; he lay in bed, trying to persuade himself that his self-control had been admirable and at the same time cursing his absence of courage in not carrying out what he had intended.

He remembered a lecture he had given Marjorie once on the subject of Sacred and Profane Love. Poor girl, how had she listened in patience ? He could see her attending with such a serious expression on her face that she looked quite ugly. She looked so beautiful when she was laughing or happy; at the Whites', for instance, three nights ago, when George and she had danced after dinner and he had sat, secretly envious, reading a book in the corner of the room and looking superior. He wouldn't learn to dance, but always wished he could. It was a barbarous, aphrodisiacal occupation, he said, and he preferred to spend his time and energies in reading. Salvationist again! What a much wiser person George had proved himself than he. He had no prejudices, no theoretical views about the conduct of life; he just lived, admirably, naturally, as the spirit or the flesh moved him. If only he could live his life again, if only he could abolish this evening's monstrous stupidity. . . .

Marjorie also lay awake. She too felt herself distorted with misery. How odiously cruel he had been, and how much she longed to forgive him! Perhaps he would come in the dark, when all the house was asleep, tiptoeing into the room very quietly to kneel by her bed and ask to be forgiven. Would he come, she wondered ? She stared into the blackness above her and about her, willing him to come, commanding him— angry and wretched because he was so slow in coming, because he didn't come at all. They were both of them asleep before two.

Seven hours of sleep make a surprising difference to the state of mind. Guy, who thought he was distorted for life, woke to find himself healthily normal. Marjorie's angers and despairs had subsided. The hour they had together between breakfast and Guy's departure was filled with almost trivial conversation. Guy was determined to say something about last's night incident. But it was only at the very last moment, when the dog-cart was actually at the door, that he managed to bring out some stammered repentance for what had happened last night.

"Don't think about it," Marjorie had told him. So they had kissed and parted, and their relations were precisely the

same as they had been before Guy came
on leave.

George was sent out a week or two
later, and a month after that they heard
at Blaybury that he had lost a leg—fortun-
ately below the knee.

"Poor boy!" said Mr. Petherton.
"I must really write a line to his mother
at once."

Jacobsen made no comment, but it
was a surprise to him to find how much
he had been moved by the news. George
White had lost a leg; he couldn't get
the thought out of his head. But only
below the knee; he might be called
lucky. Lucky — things are deplorably
relative, he reflected. One thanks God
because He has thought fit to deprive one
of His creatures of a limb.

"Neither delighteth He in any man's
legs," eh? Nous avons changé tout
cela.

George had lost a leg. There would
be no more of that Olympian speed and
strength and beauty. Jacobsen conjured
up before his memory a vision of the boy
running with his great fawn-coloured

dog across green expanses of grass. How
glorious he had looked, his fine brown
hair blowing like fire in the wind of his
own speed, his cheeks flushed, his eyes
very bright. And how easily he ran,
with long, bounding strides, looking
down at the dog that jumped and
barked at his side !

He had had a perfection, and now it
was spoilt. Instead of a leg he had a
stump. *Moignon*, the French called it ;
there was the right repulsive sound about
moignon which was lacking in " stump."
Soignons le moignon en l'oignant d'oignons.

Often, at night before he went to
sleep, he couldn't help thinking of George
and the war and all the millions of
moignons there must be in the world.
He had a dream one night of slimy red
knobbles, large polyp-like things, growing
as he looked at them, swelling between
his hands—*moignons*, in fact.

George was well enough in the late
autumn to come home. He had learnt
to hop along on his crutches very skil-
fully, and his preposterous donkey-drawn
bath-chair soon became a familiar object
in the lanes of the neighbourhood. It

was a grand sight to behold when George rattled past at the trot, leaning forward like a young Phœbus in his chariot and urging his unwilling beast with voice and crutch. He drove over to Blaybury almost every day ; Marjorie and he had endless talks about life and love and Guy and other absorbing topics. With Jacobsen he played piquet and discussed a thousand subjects. He was always gay and happy—that was what especially lacerated Jacobsen's heart with pity.

IV

THE Christmas holidays had begun, and the Reverend Roger was back again at Blaybury. He was sitting at the writing-table in the drawing-room, engaged, at the moment, in biting the end of his pen and scratching his head. His face wore an expression of perplexity ; one would have said that he was in the throes of literary composition. Which indeed he was : "Beloved ward of Alfred Petherton . . ." he said aloud. "Beloved ward . . ." He shook his head doubtfully.

The door opened and Jacobsen came into the room. Roger turned round at once.

" Have you heard the grievous news ? " he said.

" No. What ? "

" Poor Guy is dead. We got the telegram half an hour ago."

" Good God ! " said Jacobsen in an agonized voice which seemed to show that he had been startled out of the calm belonging to one who leads the life of reason. He had been conscious ever since George's mutilation that his defences were growing weaker ; external circumstance was steadily encroaching upon him. Now it had broken in and, for the moment, he was at its mercy. Guy dead. . . . He pulled himself together sufficiently to say, after a pause, " Well, I suppose it was only to be expected sooner or later. Poor boy."

" Yes, it's terrible, isn't it ? " said Roger, shaking his head. " I am just writing out an announcement to send to the *Times*. One can hardly say ' the beloved ward of Alfred Petherton,' can one ? It doesn't sound quite right ;

and yet one would like somehow to give public expression to the deep affection Alfred felt for him. ' Beloved ward '— no, decidedly it won't do.''

" You'll have to get round it somehow," said Jacobsen. Roger's presence somehow made a return to the life of reason easier.

"Poor Alfred," the other went on. " You've no idea how hardly he takes it. He feels as though he had given a son.''

"What a waste it is!" Jacobsen exclaimed. He was altogether too deeply moved.

" I have done my best to console Alfred. One must always bear in mind for what Cause he died.''

" All those potentialities destroyed. He was an able fellow, was Guy.'' Jacobsen was speaking more to himself than to his companion, but Roger took up the suggestion.

"Yes, he certainly was that. Alfred thought he was very promising. It is for his sake I am particularly sorry. I never got on very well with the boy myself. He was too eccentric for my taste. There's such a thing as being too clever, isn't there? It's rather inhuman. He used to do most remarkable Greek iambics for me when he was a boy. I dare say he was a very good fellow under all that cleverness and queerness. It's all very distressing, very grievous."

"How was he killed?"

"Died of wounds yesterday morning. Do you think it would be a good thing to put in some quotation at the end of the announcement in the paper? Something like, 'Dulce et Decorum,' or 'Sed Miles, sed Pro Patria,' or 'Per Ardua ad Astra'?"

"It hardly seems essential," said Jacobsen.

"Perhaps not." Roger's lips moved silently; he was counting. "Forty-two words. I suppose that counts as eight lines. Poor Marjorie! I hope she won't feel it too bitterly. Alfred told me they were unofficially engaged."

"So I gathered."

"I am afraid I shall have to break the news to her. Alfred is too much upset to be able to do anything himself. It will be a most painful task. Poor girl! I suppose as a matter of fact they would not have been able to marry for some time, as Guy had next to no money. These early marriages are very rash. Let me see : eight times three shillings is one pound four, isn't it ? I suppose they take cheques all right ? "

" How old was he ? " asked Jacobsen.

" Twenty-four and a few months."

Jacobsen was walking restlessly up and down the room. " Just reaching maturity ! One is thankful these days to have one's own work and thoughts to take the mind off these horrors."

" It's terrible, isn't it ?—terrible. So many of my pupils have been killed now that I can hardly keep count of the number."

There was a tapping at the French window ; it was Marjorie asking to be let in. She had been cutting holly and ivy for the Christmas decorations, and carried a basket full of dark, shining leaves.

Jacobsen unbolted the big window and Marjorie came in, flushed with the cold and smiling. Jacobsen had never seen her looking so handsome : she was superb, radiant, like Iphigenia coming in her wedding garments to the sacrifice.

" The holly is very poor this year," she

remarked. " I am afraid we shan't make much of a show with our Christmas decorations."

Jacobsen took the opportunity of slipping out through the French window. Although it was unpleasantly cold, he walked up and down the flagged paths of the Dutch garden, hatless and overcoatless, for quite a long time.

Marjorie moved about the drawing-room fixing sprigs of holly round the picture frames. Her uncle watched her, hesitating to speak ; he was feeling enormously uncomfortable.

" I am afraid," he said at last, " that your father's very upset this morning." His voice was husky ; he made an explosive noise to clear his throat.

" Is it his palpitations ? " Marjorie asked coolly ; her father's infirmities did not cause her much anxiety.

" No, no." Roger realized that his opening gambit had been a mistake. " No. It is—er—a more mental affliction, and one which, I fear, will touch you closely too. Marjorie, you must be strong and courageous ; we have just heard that Guy is dead."

"Guy dead ? " She couldn't believe it ; she had hardly envisaged the possibility ; besides, he was on the Staff. "Oh, Uncle Roger, it isn't true."

"I am afraid there is no doubt. The War Office telegram came just after you had gone out for the holly."

Marjorie sat down on the sofa and hid her face in her hands. Guy dead ; she would never see him again, never see him again, never ; she began to cry.

Roger approached and stood, with his hand on her shoulder, in the attitude of a thought-reader. To those overwhelmed by sorrow the touch of a friendly hand is often comforting. They have fallen into an abyss, and the touching hand serves to remind them that life and God and human sympathy still exist, however bottomless the gulf of grief may seem. On Marjorie's shoulder her uncle's hand rested with a damp, heavy warmth that was peculiarly unpleasant.

"Dear child, it is very grievous, I know ; but you must try and be strong and bear it bravely. We all have our cross to bear. We shall be celebrating the Birth of Christ in two days' time ; remember with what patience He received the cup of agony. And then remember for what Cause Guy has given his life. He has died a hero's death, a martyr's death, witnessing to Heaven against the powers of evil." Roger was unconsciously slipping into the words of his last sermon in the school chapel. "You should feel pride in his death as well as sorrow. There, there, poor child." He patted her shoulder two or three times. "Perhaps it would be kinder to leave you now."

For some time after her uncle's departure Marjorie sat motionless in the same position, her body bent forward, her face in her hands. She kept on repeating the words, "Never again," and the sound of them filled her with despair and made her cry. They seemed to open up such a dreary grey infinite vista— "never again." They were as a spell evoking tears.

She got up at last and began walking aimlessly about the room. She paused in front of a little old black-framed mirror that hung near the window and looked at her reflection in the glass. She had expected somehow to look different, to have

13

changed. She was surprised to find her face entirely unaltered : grave, melancholy perhaps, but still the same face she had looked at when she was doing her hair this morning. A curious idea entered her head ; she wondered whether she would be able to smile now, at this dreadful moment. She moved the muscles of her face and was overwhelmed with shame at the sight of the mirthless grin that mocked her from the glass. What a beast she was ! She burst into tears and threw herself again on the sofa, burying her face in a cushion. The door opened, and by the noise of shuffling and tapping Marjorie recognized the approach of George White on his crutches. She did not look up. At the sight of the abject figure on the sofa, George halted, uncertain what he should do. Should he quietly go away again, or should he stay and try to say something comforting ? The sight of her lying there gave him almost physical pain. He decided to stay.

He approached the sofa and stood over her, suspended on his crutches. Still she did not lift her head, but pressed her face deeper into the smothering blindness of the cushion, as though to shut out from her consciousness all the external world. George looked down at her in silence. The little delicate tendrils of hair on the nape of her neck were exquisitely beautiful.

"I was told about it," he said at last, "just now, as I came in. It's too awful. I think I cared for Guy more than for almost anyone in the world. We both did, didn't we?"

She began sobbing again. George was overcome with remorse, feeling that he had somehow hurt her, somehow added to her pain by what he had said. "Poor child, poor child," he said, almost aloud. She was a year older than he, but she seemed so helplessly and pathetically young now that she was crying.

Standing up for long tired him, and he lowered himself, slowly and painfully, into the sofa beside her. She looked up at last and began drying her eyes.

"I'm so wretched, George, so specially wretched because I feel I didn't act rightly towards darling Guy. There were times, you know, when I wondered whether it wasn't all a great mistake, our being engaged. Sometimes I felt I almost hated him. I'd been teeling so odious about him these last weeks. And now comes this, and it makes me realize how awful I've been towards him." She found it a relief to confide and confess ; George was so sympathetic, he would understand. " I've been a beast."

Her voice broke, and it was as though something had broken in George's head. He was overwhelmed with pity ; he couldn't bear it that she should suffer.

" You mustn't distress yourself un-necessarily, Marjorie dear," he begged her, stroking the back of her hand with his large hard palm. " Don't."

Marjorie went on remorselessly. "When Uncle Roger told me just now, do you know what I did ? I said to myself, Do I really care ? I couldn't make out. I looked in the glass to see if I could tell from my face. Then I suddenly thought I'd see whether I could laugh, and I did. And that made me feel how detestable I was, and I started crying again. Oh, I have been a beast, George, haven't I ? "

She burst into a passion of tears and hid her face once more in the friendly cushion. George couldn't bear it at all. He laid his hand on her shoulder and bent forward, close to her, till his face almost touched her hair. "Don't," he cried. "Don't, Marjorie. You mustn't torment yourself like this. I know you loved Guy; we both loved him. He would have wanted us to be happy and brave and to go on with life— not make his death a source of hopeless despair." There was a silence, broken only by the agonizing sound of sobbing. "Marjorie, darling, you mustn't cry."

"There, I'm not," said Marjorie through her tears. "I'll try to stop. Guy wouldn't have wanted us to cry for him. You're right; he would have wanted us to live for him—worthily, in his splendid way."

"We who knew him and loved him must make our lives a memorial of him." In ordinary circumstances George would have died rather than make a remark like that. But in speaking of the dead, people forget themselves and conform to the peculiar obituary convention of thought and language. Spontaneously, unconsciously, George had conformed.

Marjorie wiped her eyes. "Thank you, George. You know so well what darling Guy would have liked. You've made me feel stronger to bear it. But, all the same, I do feel odious for what I thought about him sometimes. I didn't love him enough. And now it's too late. I shall never see him again." The spell of that "never" worked again : Marjorie sobbed despairingly.

George's distress knew no bounds. He put his arm round Marjorie's shoulders and kissed her hair. "Don't cry, Marjorie. Everybody feels like that sometimes, even towards the people they love most. You really mustn't make yourself miserable."

Once more she lifted her face and looked at him with a heart-breaking, tearful smile. "You have been too sweet to me, George. I don't know what I should have done without you."

"Poor darling!" said George. "I can't bear to see you unhappy." Their faces were close to one another, and it seemed natural that at this point their lips should meet in a long kiss. "We'll remember only the splendid, glorious things about Guy," he went on— "what a wonderful person he was, and how much we loved him." He kissed her again.

"Perhaps our darling Guy is with us here even now," said Marjorie, with a look of ecstasy on her face.

"Perhaps he is," George echoed.

It was at this point that a heavy foot-step was heard and a hand rattled at the door. Marjorie and George moved a little farther apart. The intruder was Roger, who bustled in, rubbing his hands with an air of conscious heartiness, studiously pretending that nothing untoward had occurred. It is our English tradition that we should conceal our emotions. "Well, well," he said. "I think we had better be going in to luncheon. The bell has gone."

EUPOMPUS GAVE SPLENDOUR
TO ART BY NUMBERS

" I HAVE made a discovery," said
Emberlin as I entered his room.
" What about ? " I asked.

" A discovery," he replied, " about *Dis-coveries.*" He radiated an unconcealed
satisfaction ; the conversation had evi-
dently gone exactly as he had intended
it to go. He had made his phrase, and,
repeating it lovingly—" A discovery about
Discoveries "—he smiled benignly at me,
enjoying my look of mystification—
an expression which, I confess, I had
purposely exaggerated in order to give
him pleasure. For Emberlin, in many
ways so childish, took an especial
delight in puzzling and nonplussing his
acquaintances ; and these small triumphs,
these little " scores " off people afforded
him some of his keenest pleasures. I
always indulged his weakness when I

could, for it was worth while being on Emberlin's good books. To be allowed to listen to his post-prandial conversation was a privilege indeed. Not only was he himself a consummately good talker, but he had also the power of stimulating others to talk well. He was like some subtle wine, intoxicating just to the Meredithian level of tipsiness. In his company you would find yourself lifted to the sphere of nimble and mercurial conceptions ; you would suddenly realize that some miracle had occurred, that you were living no longer in a dull world of jumbled things but somewhere above the hotch-potch in a glassily perfect universe of ideas, where all was informed, consistent, symmetrical. And it was Emberlin who, godlike, had the power of creating this new and real world. He built it out of words, this crystal Eden, where no belly-going snake, devourer of quotidian dirt, might ever enter and disturb its harmonies. Since I first knew Emberlin I have come to have a greatly enhanced respect for magic and all the formules of its liturgy. If by words Emberlin can create a new world for me, can make my spirit slough off completely the domination of the old, why should not he or I or anyone, having found the suitable phrases, exert by means of them an influence more vulgarly miraculous upon the world of mere things ? Indeed, when I compare Emberlin and the common or garden black magician of commerce, it seems to me that Emberlin is the greater thaumaturge. But let that pass ; I am straying from my purpose, which was to give some description of the man who so confidentially whispered to me that he had made a discovery about *Discoveries.*

In the best sense of the word, then, Emberlin was academic. For us who knew him his rooms were an oasis of aloofness planted secretly in the heart of the desert of London. He exhaled an atmosphere that combined the fantastic speculativeness of the undergraduate with the more mellowed oddity of incredibly wise and antique dons. He was immensely erudite, but in a wholly unencyclopædic way—a mine of irrelevant information, as his enemies said of him. He wrote a certain amount, but, like Mallarmé, avoided publication, deeming it akin to " the offence of exhibitionism." Once, however, in the folly of youth, some dozen years ago, he had published a volume of verses. He spent a good deal of time now in assiduously collecting copies of his book and burning them. There can be but very few left in the world now. My friend Cope had the fortune to pick one up the other day—a little blue book, which he showed me very secretly. I am at a loss to understand why Emberlin wishes to stamp out all trace of it. There is nothing to be ashamed of in the book ; some of the verses, indeed, are, in their young ecstatic fashion, good. But they are certainly conceived in a style that is unlike that of his present poems. Perhaps it is that which makes him so implacable against them. What he writes now for very private manuscript circulation is curious stuff. I confess I prefer the earlier work ; I do not like the stony, hard-edged quality of this sort of thing—the only one I can remember of his later productions. It is a sonnet on a porcelain figure of a woman, dug up at Cnossus :

> " Her eyes of bright unwinking glaze
> All imperturbable do not
> Even make pretences to regard
> The jutting absence of her stays
> Where many a Syrian gallipot
> Excites desire with spilth of nard.
> The bistred rims above the fard
> Of cheeks as red as bergamot
> Attest that no shamefaced delays
> Will clog fulfilment nor retard
> Full payment of the Cyprian's praise
> Down to the last remorseful jot.
> Hail priestess of we know not what
> Strange cult of Mycenean days ! "

Regrettably, I cannot remember any of Emberlin's French poems. His peculiar muse expresses herself better, I think, in that language than in her native tongue.

Such is Emberlin ; such, I should rather say, *was* he, for, as I propose to show, he is not now the man that he was when he whispered so confidentially to me, as I entered the room, that he had made a discovery about *Discoveries*.

I waited patiently till he had finished his little game of mystification and, when the moment seemed ripe, I asked him to

explain himself. Emberlin was ready to
open out.

"Well," he began, "these are the
facts—a tedious introduction, I fear, but
necessary. Years ago, when I was first
reading Ben Jonson's *Discoveries*, that
queer jotting of his, 'Eupompus gave
splendour to Art by Numbers,' tickled
my curiosity. You yourself must have
been struck by the phrase, everybody
must have noticed it; and everybody
must have noticed too that no com-
mentator has a word to say on the subject.
That is the way of commentators—the
obvious points fulsomely explained and
discussed, the hard passages, about which
one might want to know something passed
over in the silence of sheer ignorance.
'Eupompus gave splendour to Art by
Numbers'—the absurd phrase stuck in my
head. At one time it positively haunted
me. I used to chant it in my bath, set
to music as an anthem. It went like this,
so far as I remember"—and he burst
into song: "'Eupompus, Eu-u-pompus
gave sple-e-e-endour . . .'" and so on,
through all the repetitions, the dragged-
out rises and falls of a parodied anthem.

" I sing you this," he said when he had finished, " just to show you what a hold that dreadful sentence took upon my mind. For eight years, off and on, its senselessness has besieged me. I have looked up Eupompus in all the obvious books of reference, of course. He is there all right—Alexandrian artist, eternized by some wretched little author in some even wretcheder little anecdote, which at the moment I entirely forget ; it had nothing, at any rate, to do with the embellishment of art by numbers. Long ago I gave up the search as hopeless ; Eupompus remained for me a shadowy figure of mystery, author of some nameless outrage, bestower of some forgotten benefit upon the art that he practised. His history seemed wrapt in an impenetrable darkness. And then yesterday I discovered all about him and his art and his numbers. A chance discovery, than which few things have given me a greater pleasure.

" I happened upon it, as I say, yesterday when I was glancing through a volume of Zuylerius. Not, of course, the Zuylerius one knows," he added quickly, " otherwise one would have had the heart out of Eupompus' secret years ago."

"Of course," I repeated, "not the familiar Zuylerius."

"Exactly," said Emberlin, taking seriously my flippancy, "not the familiar John Zuylerius, Junior, but the elder Henricus Zuylerius, a much less—though perhaps undeservedly so — renowned figure than his son. But this is not the time to discuss their respective merits. At any rate, I discovered in a volume of critical dialogues by the elder Zuylerius, the reference, to which, without doubt, Jonson was referring in his note. (It was of course a mere jotting, never meant to be printed, but which Jonson's literary executors pitched into the book with all the rest of the available posthumous materials.) 'Eupompus gave splendour to Art by Numbers'—Zuylerius gives a very circumstantial account of the process. He must, I suppose, have found the sources for it in some writer now lost to us."

Emberlin paused a moment to muse. The loss of the work of any ancient writer gave him the keenest sorrow. I rather believe he had written a version of the unrecovered books of Petronius. Some day I hope I shall be permitted to see what conception Emberlin has of the *Satyricon* as a whole. He would, I am sure, do Petronius justice—almost too much, perhaps.

"What was the story of Eupompus?" I asked. "I am all curiosity to know."

Emberlin heaved a sigh and went on.

"Zuylerius' narrative," he said, "is very bald, but on the whole lucid; and I think it gives one the main points of the story. I will give it you in my own words; that is preferable to reading his Dutch Latin. Eupompus, then, was one of the most fashionable portrait-painters of Alexandria. His clientele was large, his business immensely profitable. For a half-length in oils the great courtesans would pay him a month's earnings. He would paint likenesses of the merchant princes in exchange for the costliest of their outlandish treasures. Coal-black potentates would come a thousand miles out of Ethiopia to have a miniature limned on some specially choice panel of ivory; and for payment there would be camel-loads of gold and spices. Fame, riches, and honour came to him while he was yet young ; an unparalleled career seemed to lie before him. And then, quite suddenly, he gave it all up—refused to paint another portrait. The doors of his studio were closed. It was in vain that clients, however rich, however distinguished, demanded admission ; the slaves had their order ; Eupompus would see no one but his own intimates."

Emberlin made a pause in his narrative.

" What was Eupompus doing ? " I asked.

" He was, of course," said Emberlin, " occupied in giving splendour to Art by Numbers. And this, as far as I can gather from Zuylerius, is how it all happened. He just suddenly fell in love with numbers—head over ears, amorous of pure counting. Number seemed to him to be the sole reality, the only thing about which the mind of man could be certain. To count was the one thing worth doing, because it was the one thing you could be sure of doing right. Thus, art, that it may have any value at all, must ally itself with reality—must,

14

that is, possess a numerical foundation. He carried the idea into practice by painting the first picture in his new style. It was a gigantic canvas, covering several hundred square feet—I have no doubt that Eupompus could have told you the exact area to an inch—and upon it was represented an illimitable ocean covered, as far as the eye could reach in every direction, with a multitude of black swans. There were thirty-three thousand of these black swans, each, even though it might be but a speck on the horizon, distinctly limned. In the middle of the ocean was an island, upon which stood a more or less human figure having three eyes, three arms and legs, three breasts and three navels. In the leaden sky three suns were dimly expiring. There was nothing more in the picture ; Zuylerius describes it exactly. Eupompus spent nine months of hard work in painting it. The privileged few who were allowed to see it pronounced it, finished, a masterpiece. They gathered round Eupompus in a little school, calling themselves the Philarithmics. They would sit for hours in front of his great work, contemplating the swans and counting them ; according to the Philarithmics, to count and to contemplate were the same thing.

Eupompus' next picture, representing an orchard of identical trees set in quincunxes, was regarded with less favour by the connoisseurs. His studies of crowds were, however, more highly esteemed ; in these were portrayed masses of people arranged in groups that exactly imitated the number and position of the stars making up various of the more famous constellations. And then there was his famous picture of the amphitheatre, which created a furore among the Philarithmics. Zuylerius again gives us a detailed description. Tier upon tier of seats are seen, all occupied by strange Cyclopean figures. Each tier accommodates more people than the tier below, and the number rises in a complicated but regular progression. All the figures seated in the amphitheatre possess but a single eye, enormous and luminous, planted in the middle of the forehead : and all these thousands of single eyes are fixed, in a terrible and menacing scrutiny, upon a dwarf-like creature cowering pitiably in the arena. . . . He alone of the multitude possesses two eyes.

"I would give anything to see that picture," Emberlin added, after a pause. "The colouring, you know; Zuylerius gives no hint, but I feel somehow certain that the dominant tone must have been a fierce brick-red—a red granite amphitheatre filled with a red-robed assembly, sharply defined against an implacable blue sky."

"Their eyes would be green," I suggested.

Emberlin closed his eyes to visualize the scene and then nodded a slow and rather dubious assent.

"Up to this point," Emberlin resumed at length, "Zuylerius' account is very clear. But his descriptions of the later philarithmic art become extremely obscure; I doubt whether he understood in the least what it was all about. I will give you such meaning as I manage to extract from his chaos. Eupompus seems to have grown tired of painting merely numbers of objects. He wanted now to represent Number itself. And then he conceived the plan of rendering visible the fundamental ideas of life through the medium of those purely numerical terms into which, according to him, they must ultimately resolve themselves. Zuylerius speaks vaguely of a picture of Eros, which seems to have consisted of a series of interlacing planes. Eupompus' fancy seems next to have been taken by various of the Socratic dialogues upon the nature of general ideas, and he made a series of illustrations for them in the same arithmogeometric style. Finally there is Zuylerius' wild description of the last picture that Eupompus ever painted. I can make very little of it. The subject of the work, at least, is clearly stated; it was a representation of Pure Number, or God and the Universe, or whatever you like to call that pleasingly inane conception of totality. It was a picture of the cosmos seen, I take it, through a rather Neoplatonic *camera obscura* — very clear and in small. Zuylerius suggests a design of planes radiating out from a single point of light. I dare

say something of the kind came in
Actually, I have no doubt, the work was
a very adequate rendering in visible form
of the conception of the one and the
many, with all the intermediate stages of
enlightenment between matter and the
Fons Deitatis. However, it's no use
speculating what the picture may have
been going to look like. Poor old
Eupompus went mad before he had
completely finished it and, after he had
dispatched two of the admiring Philarithmics with a hammer, he flung himself out of the window and broke his
neck. That was the end of him, and
that was how he gave splendour, regrettably transient, to Art by Numbers."

Emberlin stopped. We brooded over
our pipes in silence ; poor old Eupompus !

That was four months ago, and to-day
Emberlin is a confirmed and apparently
irreclaimable Philarithmic, a quite whole-
hearted Eupompian.

It was always Emberlin's way to take
up the ideas that he finds in books and
to put them into practice. He was once,

for example, a working alchemist, and attained to considerable proficiency in the Great Art. He studied mnemonics under Bruno and Raymond Lully, and constructed for himself a model of the latter's syllogizing machine, in hopes of gaining that universal knowledge which the Enlightened Doctor guaranteed to its user. This time it is Eupompianism, and the thing has taken hold of him. I have held up to him all the hideous warnings that I can find in history. But it is no use.

There is the pitiable spectacle of Dr. Johnson under the tyranny of an Eupompian ritual, counting the posts and the paving-stones of Fleet Street. He himself knew best how nearly a madman he was.

And then I count as Eupompians all gamblers, all calculating boys, all interpreters of the prophecies of Daniel and the Apocalypse ; then too the Elberfeld horses, most complete of all Eupompians.

And here was Emberlin joining himself to this sect, degrading himself to the level of counting beasts and irrational children and men, more or less insane.

Dr. Johnson was at least born with a strain of the Eupompian aberration in him ; Emberlin is busily and consciously acquiring it. My expostulations, the expostulations of all his friends, are as yet unavailing. It is in vain that I tell Emberlin that counting is the easiest thing in the world to do, that when I am utterly exhausted, my brain, for lack of ability to perform any other work, just counts and reckons, like a machine, like an Elberfeld horse. It all falls on deaf ears ; Emberlin merely smiles and shows me some new numerical joke that he has discovered. Emberlin can never enter a tiled bathroom now without counting how many courses of tiles there are from floor to ceiling. He regards it as an interesting fact that there are twenty-six rows of tiles in his bathroom and thirty-two in mine, while all the public lavatories in Holborn have the same number. He knows now how many paces it is from any one point in London to any other. I have given up going for walks with him. I am always made so distressingly conscious by his preoccupied look, that he is counting his steps.

His evenings, too, have become profoundly melancholy ; the conversation, however well it may begin, always comes round to the same nauseating subject. We can never escape numbers ; Eupompus haunts us. It is not as if we were mathematicians and could discuss problems of any interest or value. No, none of us are mathematicians, least of all Emberlin. Emberlin likes talking about such points as the numerical significance of the Trinity, the immense importance of its being three in one, not forgetting the even greater importance of its being one in three. He likes giving us statistics about the speed of light or the rate of growth in finger-nails. He loves to speculate on the nature of odd and even numbers. And he seems to be unconscious how much he has changed for the worse. He is happy in an exclusively absorbing interest. It is as though some mental leprosy had fallen upon his intelligence.

In another year or so, I tell Emberlin, he may almost be able to compete with the calculating horses on their own ground. He will have lost all traces of his reason, but he will be able to extract cube roots in his head. It occurs to me that the reason why Eupompus killed himself was not that he was mad; on the contrary, it was because he was, temporarily, sane. He had been mad for years, and then suddenly the idiot's self-complacency was lit up by a flash of sanity. By its momentary light he saw into what gulfs of imbecility he had plunged. He saw and understood, and the full horror, the lamentable absurdity of the situation made him desperate. He vindicated Eupompus against Eupompianism, humanity against the Philarithmics. It gives me the greatest pleasure to think that he disposed of two of that hideous crew before he died himself.

HAPPY FAMILIES

THE scene is a conservatory. Luxuriant tropical plants are seen looming through a greenish aquarium twilight, punctuated here and there by the surprising pink of several Chinese lanterns hanging from the roof or on the branches of trees, while a warm yellow radiance streams out from the ball-room by a door on the left of the scene. Through the glass of the conservatory, at the back of the stage, one perceives a black-and-white landscape under the moon —expanses of snow, lined and dotted with coal-black hedges and trees. Outside is frost and death : but within the conservatory all is palpitating and steaming with tropical life and heat. Enormous fantastic plants encumber it ; trees, creepers that writhe with serpentine life, orchids of every kind. Everywhere dense vegetation ; horrible flowers that look like bottled spiders, like suppurating wounds ;

flowers with eyes and tongues, with moving, sensitive tentacles, with breasts and teeth and spotted skins.

The strains of a waltz float in through the ball-room door, and to that slow, soft music there enter, in parallel processions, the two families which are respectively Mr. Aston J. Tyrrell and Miss Topsy Garrick.

The doyen of the Tyrrell family is a young and perhaps too cultured literary man with rather long, dark brown hair, a face well cut and sensitive, if a trifle weak about the lower jaw, and a voice whose exquisite modulations could only be the product of education at one of the two Great Universities. We will call him plain Aston. Miss Topsy, the head of the Garrick family, is a young woman of not quite twenty, with sleek, yellow hair hanging, like a page's, short and thick about her ears; boyish, too, in her slenderness and length of leg—boyish, but feminine and attractive to the last degree. Miss Topsy paints charmingly, sings in a small, pure voice that twists the heart and makes the bowels yearn in the hearing of it, is well educated and has read, or at least heard of, most of the best books in three languages, knows something, too, of economics and the doctrines of Freud.

They enter arm in arm, fresh from the dance, trailing behind them with their disengaged hands two absurd ventriloquist's dummies of themselves. They sit down on a bench placed in the middle of the stage under a kind of arbour festooned with fabulous flowers. The other members of the two families lurk in the tropical twilight of the background.

Aston advances his dummy and makes it speak, moving its mouth and limbs appropriately by means of the secret levers which his hand controls.

Aston's Dummy.

What a perfect floor it is to-night !

Topsy's Dummy.

Yes, it's like ice, isn't it ? And such a good band.

Aston's Dummy.

Oh yes, a very good band.

Topsy's Dummy.

They play at dinner - time **at** the Necropole, you know.

Aston's Dummy.

Really! (*A long, uncomfortable silence.*)
(*From under a lofty twangum tree emerges the figure of* CAIN WASHINGTON TYRRELL, ASTON'S *negro brother—for the* TYRRELLS, *I regret to say, have a lick of the tar-brush in them and* CAIN *is a Mendelian throwback to the pure Jamaican type.* CAIN *is stout and his black face shines with grease. The whites of his eyes are like enamel, his smile is chryselephantine. He is dressed in faultless evening dress and a ribbon of seals tinkles on his stomach. He walks with legs wide apart, the upper part of his body thrown back and his belly projecting, as though he were supporting the weight of an Aristophanic*

*actor's costume. He struts up
and down in front of the couple
on the seat, grinning and
slapping himself on the waistcoat.*)

CAIN.

What hair, nyum nyum! and the
nape of her neck; and her body—how
slender! and what lovely movements,
nyum nyum! (*Approaching* ASTON *and
speaking into his ear.*) Eh? eh? eh?

ASTON.

Go away, you pig. Go away. (*He
holds up his dummy as a shield:* CAIN
retires discomfited.)

ASTON'S DUMMY.

Have you read any amusing novels
lately?

TOPSY.

(*Speaking over the head of her dummy.*)
No; I never read novels. They are
mostly so frightful, aren't they?

ASTON.

(*Enthusiastically.*) How splendid! Neither do I. I only write them sometimes, that's all. (*They abandon their dummies, which fall limply into one another's arms and collapse on to the floor with an expiring sigh.*)

TOPSY.

You write them? I didn't know. . . .

ASTON.

Oh, I'd very much rather you didn't know. I shouldn't like you ever to read one of them. They're all awful: still, they keep the pot boiling, you know. But tell me, what do you read?

TOPSY.

Mostly history, and philosophy, and a little criticism and psychology, and lots of poetry.

ASTON.

My dear young lady! how wonderful, how altogether unexpectedly splendid.

(CAIN *emerges with the third brother,* SIR JASPER, *who is a paler, thinner, more sinister and aristocratic* ASTON.)

CAIN.

Nyum nyum nyum. . . .

SIR JASPER.

What a perfect sentence that was of yours, Aston : quite Henry Jamesian ! " My dear young lady "—as though you were forty years her senior ; and the rare old-worldliness of that " altogether unexpectedly splendid " ! Admirable. I don't remember your ever employing quite exactly this opening gambit before : but of course there were things very like it. (*To* CAIN.) What a nasty spectacle you are, Cain, gnashing your teeth like that !

CAIN.

Nyum nyum nyum.
(ASTON *and* TOPSY *are enthusiastically talking about books :*

15

the two brothers, finding themselves quite unnoticed, retire into the shade of their twangum tree. BELLE GARRICK *has been hovering behind* TOPSY *for some time past. She is more obviously pretty than her sister, full-bosomed and with a loose, red, laughing mouth. Unable to attract* TOPSY'S *attention, she turns round and calls, "* HENRIKA.*" A pale face with wide, surprised eyes peeps round the trunk, hairy like a mammoth's leg, of a kadapoo tree with magenta leaves and flame-coloured blossoms. This is* HENRIKA, TOPSY'S *youngest sister. She is dressed in a little white muslin frock set off with blue ribbons.)*

HENRIKA.

(Tiptoes forward.) Here I am; what is it? I was rather frightened of that man. But he really seems quite nice and tame, doesn't he?

BELLE.

Of course he is ! What a goose you are
to hide like that !

HENRIKA.

He seems a nice, quiet, gentle man ;
and *so* clever.

BELLE.

What good hands he has, hasn't he ?
(*Approaching* TOPSY *and whispering in her
ear.*) Your hair's going into your eyes,
my dear. Toss it back in that pretty way
you have. (TOPSY *tosses her head ; the
soft, golden bell of hair quivers elastically
about her ears.*) That's right !

CAIN.

(*Bounding into the air and landing with
feet apart, knees bent, and a hand on either
knee.*) Oh, nyum nyum !

ASTON.

Oh, the beauty of that movement !
It simply makes one catch one's breath

with surprised pleasure, as the gesture of
a perfect dancer might.

SIR JASPER.

Beautiful, wasn't it ?—a pleasure purely
æsthetic and æsthetically pure. Listen
to Cain.

ASTON.

(*To* TOPSY.) And do you ever try
writing yourself ? I'm sure you ought
to.

SIR JASPER.

Yes, yes, we're sure you ought to. Eh,
Cain ?

TOPSY.

Well, I have written a little poetry—or
rather a few bad verses—at one time or
another.

ASTON.

Really **now** ! What about, may I ask ?

TOPSY.

Well . . . (*hesitating*) about different things, you know. (*She fans herself rather nervously.*)

BELLE.

(*Leaning over* TOPSY's *shoulder and addressing* ASTON *directly.*) Mostly about Love. (*She dwells long and voluptuously on the last word, pronouncing it " lovv " rather than " luvv."*)

CAIN.

Oh, dat's good, dat's good ; dat's dam good. (*In moments of emotion* CAIN's *manners and language savour more obviously than usual of the Old Plantation.*) Did yoh see her face den ?

BELLE.

(*Repeats, slowly and solemnly.*) Mostly about Love.

HENRIKA.

Oh, oh. (*She covers her face with her hands.*) How could you ? It makes me tingle all over. (*She runs behind the kadapoo tree again.*)

Aston.

(*Very seriously and intelligently.*)
Really. That's very interesting. I wish
you'd let me see what you've done some
time.

Sir Jasper.

We always like to see these things, don't
we, Aston ? Do you remember Mrs.
Towler ? How pretty she was ! And
the way we criticized her literary productions. . . .

Aston.

Mrs. Towler. . . . (*He shudders as
though he had touched something soft and
filthy.*) Oh, don't, Jasper, don't !

Sir Jasper.

Dear Mrs. Towler ! We were very
nice about her poems, weren't we ? Do
you remember the one that began :

" My Love is like a silvern flower-de-luce
    Within some wondrous dream-garden pent :
God made my lovely lily not for use,
    But for an ornament."

Even Cain, I believe, saw the joke of that.

ASTON.

Mrs. Towler—oh, my God! But this is quite different : this girl really interests me.

SIR JASPER.

Oh yes, I know, I know. She interests you too, Cain, doesn't she ?

CAIN.

(*Prances two or three steps of a cake-walk and sings.*)   Oh, ma honey, oh, ma honey.

ASTON.

But, I tell you, this is quite different.

SIR JASPER.

Of course it is.   Any fool could see that it was.   I've admitted it already.

Aston.

(*To* Topsy.) You will show them me, won't you? I should so much like to see them.

Topsy.

(*Covered with confusion.*) No, I really couldn't. You're a professional, you see.

Henrika.

(*From behind the kadapoo tree.*) No, you mustn't show them to him. They're really mine, you know, a great many of them.

Belle.

Nonsense! (*She stoops down and moves* Topsy's *foot in such a way that a very well-shaped, white-stockinged leg is visible some way up the calf. Then, to* Topsy.) Pull your skirt down, my dear. You're quite indecent.

Cain.

(*Putting up his monocle.*) Oh, nyum nyum, ma honey! Come wid me to Dixie Land. . . .

Sir Jasper.

H'm, a little conscious, don't you think ?

Aston.

But even professionals are human, my dear young lady. And perhaps I might be able to give you some help with your writings.

Topsy.

That's awfully kind of you, Mr. Tyrrell.

Henrika.

Oh, don't let him see them. I don't want him to. Don't let him.

Aston.

(*With heavy charm.*) It always interests me so much when I hear of the young—and I trust you won't be offended if I include you in their number—when I hear of the young taking to writing. It is one of the most important duties that we of the older generation can perform—to help and encourage the young with their work. It's a great service to the cause of Art.

SIR JASPER.

That was what I was always saying to Mrs. Towler, if I remember rightly.

TOPSY.

I can't tell you, Mr. Tyrrell, how delightful it is to have one's work taken seriously. I am so grateful to you. May I send you my little efforts, then?

CAIN.

(*Executes a step dance to the furious clicking of a pair of bones.*)

SIR JASPER.

I congratulate you, Aston. A most masterful bit of strategy.

BELLE.

I wonder what he'll do next. Isn't it exciting? Topsy, toss your head again. That's right. Oh, I wish something would happen!

HENRIKA.

What have you done ? Oh, Topsy, you really mustn't send him my poems.

BELLE.

You said he was such a nice man just now.

HENRIKA.

Oh yes, he's nice, I know. But then he's a man, you must admit that.   I don't want him to see them.

TOPSY.

(*Firmly.*) You're being merely foolish, Henrika.   Mr. Tyrrell, a very distinguished literary man, has been kind enough to take an interest in my work. His criticism will be the greatest help to me.

BELLE.

Of course it will, and he has such charming eyes. (*A pause. The music, which has, all this while, been faintly heard through the ball-room door, becomes more audible. They are playing a rich, creamy waltz.)* What delicious music! Henrika, come and have a dance. *(She seizes* HENRIKA *round the waist and begins to waltz.* HENRIKA *is reluctant at first, but little by little the rhythm of the dance takes possession of her till, with her half-closed eyes and languorous, trance-like movements, she might figure as the visible living symbol of the waltz.* ASTON *and* TOPSY *lean back in their seats, marking the time with a languid beating of the hand.* CAIN *sways and swoons and revolves in his own peculiar and inimitable version of the dance.)*

SIR JASPER.

(Who has been watching the whole scene with amusement.) What a pretty spectacle! " Music hath charms. . . ."

HENRIKA.

(In an almost extinct voice.) Oh, Belle, Belle, I could go on dancing like this for ever. I feel quite intoxicated with it.

Topsy.

(*To* Aston.)   What a jolly tune this is !

Aston.

Isn't it? It's called " Dreams of Desire,"
I believe.

Belle.

What a pretty name !

Topsy.

These are wonderful flowers here.

Aston.

Let's go and have a look at them.
   (*They get up and walk round the
      conservatory.   The   flowers
      light up as they pass ; in the
      midst of each is a small electric
      globe.*)

Aston.

This purple one with eyes is the
assafœtida flower. Don't put your nose
too near ; it has a smell like burning flesh.

This is a Cypripedium from Sumatra. It
is the only man-eating flower in the world.
Notice its double set of teeth. (*He puts
a stick into the mouth of the flower, which
instantly snaps to, like a steel trap.*) Nasty,
vicious brute! These blossoms like
purple sponges belong to the twangum
tree; when you squeeze them they ooze
blood. This is the Jonesia, the octopus
of the floral world: each of its eight
tentacles is armed with a sting capable
of killing a horse. Now this is a most
interesting and instructive flower—the
patchouli bloom. It is perhaps the most
striking example in nature of structural
specialization brought about by Evolution.
If only Darwin had lived to see the patchouli plant! You have heard of flowers
specially adapting themselves to be
fertilized by bees or butterflies or spiders
and such-like? Well, this plant which
grows in the forests of Guatemala can only
be fertilized by English explorers. Observe the structure of the flower; at
the base is a flat, projecting pan, con-
taining the pistil; above it an over-
arching tube ending in a spout. On
either side a small crevice about three-

quarters of an inch in length may be discerned in the fleshy lobes of the calyx. The English traveller seeing this plant is immediately struck by its resemblance to those penny-in-the-slot machines which provide scent for the public in the railway stations at home. Through sheer force of habit he takes a penny from his pocket and inserts it in one of the crevices or slots. Immediate result — a jet of highly scented liquid pollen is discharged from the spout upon the pistil lying below, and the plant is fertilized. Could anything be more miraculous ? And yet there are those who deny the existence of God. Poor fools !

TOPSY.

Wonderful ! (*Sniffing.*) What a good scent.

ASTON.

The purest patchouli.

BELLE.

How delicious ! Oh, my dear . . . (*She shuts her eyes in ecstasy.*)

HENRIKA.

(*Drowsily.*) Delicious, 'licious. . . .

SIR JASPER.

I always like these rather *canaille* perfumes. Their effect is admirable.

ASTON.

This is the leopard-flower. Observe its spotted skin and its thorns like agate claws. This is the singing Alocusia—Alocusia Cantatrix—discovered by Humboldt during his second voyage to the Amazons. If you stroke its throat in the right place, it will begin to sing like a nightingale. Allow me. (*He takes her by the wrist and guides her fingers towards the palpitating throat of a gigantic flower shaped like a gramophone trumpet. The Alocusia bursts into song ; it has a voice like Caruso's.*)

CAIN.

Oh, nyum nyum ! What a hand ! Oh, ma honey. (*He runs a thick black finger along* TOPSY's *arm.*)

Topsy.

What a remarkable flower!

Belle.

I wonder whether he stroked my arm like that by accident or on purpose.

Henrika.

(*Gives a little shiver.*) He's touching me, he's touching me! But somehow I feel so sleepy I can't move.

Topsy.

(*She moves on towards the next flower :* Belle *does not allow her to disengage her hand at once.*) What a curious smell this one has!

Aston.

Be careful, be careful! That's the chloroform plant.

16

TOPSY.

Oh, I feel quite dizzy and faint.   That smell and the heat . . . (*She almost falls :* ASTON *puts out his arm and holds her up.*)

ASTON.

Poor child !

CAIN.

Poh chile, poh chile !   (*He hovers round her, his hands almost touching her, trembling with excitement :   his white eyeballs roll horribly.*)

ASTON.

I'll open the door.   The air will make you feel better. (*He opens the conservatory door, still supporting* TOPSY *with his right arm.   The wind is heard, fearfully whistling :   a flurry of snow blows into the conservatory.   The flowers utter piercing screams of rage and fear ;   their lights flicker wildly ;   several turn perfectly black and drop on to the floor writhing in agony. The floral octopus agitates its tentacles ;   the twangum blooms drip blood ;   all the leaves of all the trees clap together with a dry, scaly sound.)*

TOPSY.

(*Faintly.*) Thank you; that's better.

ASTON.

(*Closing the door.*) Poor child! Come and sit down again; the chloroform flower is a real danger. (*Much moved, he leads her back towards the seat.*)

CAIN.

(*Executes a war dance round the seated couple.*) Poh chile, poh chile! Nyum nyum nyum.

SIR JASPER.

One perceives the well-known dangers of playing the Good Samaritan towards an afflicted member of the opposite sex. Pity has touched even our good Cain to tears.

Belle.

Oh, I wonder what's going to happen! It's so exciting. I'm so glad Henrika's gone to sleep.

Topsy.

It was silly of me to go all faint like that.

Aston.

I ought to have warned you in time of the chloroform flower.

Belle.

But it's such a lovely feeling now—like being in a very hot bath with lots of verbena bath-salts, and hardly able to move with limpness, but just ever so comfortable and happy.

Aston.

How do you feel now? I'm afraid you're looking very pale. Poor child!

CAIN.

Poh chile, poh chile! . . .

SIR JASPER.

I don't know much about these things, but it seems to me, my dear Aston, that the moment has decidedly arrived.

ASTON.

I'm so sorry.   You poor little thing . . . (*He kisses her very gently on the forehead.*)

BELLE.

A—a—h.

HENRIKA.

Oh !   He kissed me : but he's so kind and good, so kind and good. (*She stirs and falls back again into her drowsy trance.*)

CAIN.

Poh chile, poh chile ! (*He leans over* ASTON's *shoulder and begins rudely kissing*

TOPSY'S *trance-calm, parted lips.* TOPSY *opens her eyes and sees the black, greasy face, the chryselephantine smile, the pink, thick lips, the goggling eyeballs of white enamel. She screams.* HENRIKA *springs up and screams too.* TOPSY *slips on to the floor, and* CAIN *and* ASTON *are left face to face with* HENRIKA, *pale as death and with wide-open, terrified eyes. She is trembling in every limb.*)

ASTON.

(*Gives* CAIN *a push that sends him sprawling backwards, and falls on his knees before the pathetic figure of* HENRIKA.) Oh, I'm so sorry, I'm so sorry. What a beast I am! I don't know what I can have been thinking of to do such a thing.

SIR JASPER.

My dear boy, I'm afraid you and Cain knew only too well what you were thinking of. Only too well . . .

ASTON.

Will you forgive me? I can't forgive myself.

Henrika.

Oh, you hurt me, you frightened me so much. I can't bear it. (*She cries.*)

Aston.

O God! O God! (*The tears start into his eyes also. He takes* Henrika's *hand and begins to kiss it.*) I'm so sorry, I'm so sorry.

Sir Jasper.

If you're not very careful, Aston, you'll have Cain to deal with again. (Cain *has picked himself up and is creeping stealthily towards the couple in the centre of the conservatory.*)

Aston.

(*Turning round.*) Cain, you brute, go to hell! (Cain *slinks back.*) Oh, will you forgive me for having been such a swine? What can I do?

TOPSY.

(*Who has recovered her self-possession, rises to her feet and pushes* HENRIKA *into the background.*) Thank you, it is really quite all right. I think it would be best to say no more about it, to forget what has happened.

ASTON.

Will you forgive me, then ?

TOPSY.

Of course, of course. Please get up Mr. Tyrrell.

ASTON.

(*Climbing to his feet.*) I can't think how I ever came to be such a brute.

TOPSY.

(*Coldly.*) I thought we had agreed not to talk about this incident any further. (*There is a silence.*)

SIR JASPER.

Well, Aston ? This has been rather
fun.

BELLE.

I wish you hadn't been quite so cold
with him, Topsy. Poor man ! He really
is very sorry. One can see that.

HENRIKA.

But did you see that awful face ?   (*She
shudders and covers her eyes.*)

ASTON.

(*Picking up his dummy and manipulating
it.*) It is very hot in here, is it not ?
Shall we go back to the dancing-room ?

TOPSY.

(*Also takes up her dummy.*) Yes, let us
go back.

ASTON'S DUMMY.

Isn't that " Roses in Picardy " that the band is playing ?

TOPSY'S DUMMY.

I believe it is.   What a very good band, don't you think ?

ASTON'S DUMMY.

Yes ; it plays during dinner, you know, at the Necropole. (*To* JASPER.)   Lord, what a fool I am !   I'd quite forgotten ; it was she who told me so as we came in.

TOPSY'S DUMMY.

At the Necropole ?   Really.

ASTON'S DUMMY.

A very good band and a very good floor.

TOPSY'S DUMMY.

Yes, it's a perfect floor, isn't it ?   Like glass. . . . (*They go out, followed by*

their respective families. BELLE *supports*
HENRIKA, *who is still very weak after her
shock.*)

BELLE.

How exciting it was, wasn't it, HENRIKA?

HENRIKA.

Wasn't it awful—too awful! Oh,
that face. . . . (CAIN *follows* ASTON *out in
silence and dejection.* SIR JASPER *brings
up the rear of the procession. His face
wears its usual expression of slightly bored
amusement. He lights a cigarette.*)

SIR JASPER.

Charming evening, charming evening.
. . . Now it's over, I wonder whether it
ever existed. (*He goes out. The conservatory is left empty. The flowers flash their
luminous pistils ; the eyes of the assafœtida blossoms solemnly wink ; leaves shake
and sway and rustle ; several of the flowers*

*are heard to utter a low chuckle, while the
Alocusia, after whistling a few derisive notes,
finally utters a loud, gross Oriental hiccough.)*

THE CURTAIN SLOWLY DESCENDS.

CYNTHIA

WHEN, some fifty years hence, my grandchildren ask me what I did when I was at Oxford in the remote days towards the beginning of our monstrous century, I shall look back across the widening gulf of time and tell them with perfect good faith that I never worked less than eight hours a day, that I took a keen interest in Social Service, and that coffee was the strongest stimulant in which I indulged. And they will very justly say—but I hope I shall be out of hearing. That is why I propose to write my memoirs as soon as possible, before I have had time to forget, so that having the truth before me I shall never in time to come be able, consciously or unconsciously, to tell lies about myself.

At present I have no time to write a complete account of that decisive period in my history. I must content myself

therefore with describing a single incident of my undergraduate days. I have
selected this one because it is curious and
at the same time wholly characteristic of
Oxford life before the war.

My friend Lykeham was an Exhibi-
tioner at Swellfoot College. He combined blood (he was immensely proud of
his Anglo-Saxon descent and the deriva-
tion of his name from Old English *lycam*,
a corpse) with brains. His tastes were
eccentric, his habits deplorable, the
range of his information immense. As
he is now dead, I will say no more about
his character.

To proceed with my anecdote : I had
gone one evening, as was my custom, to
visit him in his rooms at Swellfoot. It
was just after nine when I mounted the
stairs, and great Tom was still tolling.

> " In Thomae laude
> Resono bim bam sine fraude,"

as the charmingly imbecile motto used
to run, and to-night he was living up to
it by bim-bamming away in a persistent
basso profondo that made an astonishing
background of discord to the sound of

frantic guitar playing which emanated
from Lykeham's room. From the fury
of his twanging I could tell that something more than usually cataclysmic had
happened, for mercifully it was only in
moments of the greatest stress that
Lykeham touched his guitar.

I entered the room with my hands over
my ears. "For God's sake——" I im-
plored. Through the open window Tom
was shouting a deep E flat, with a spread
chord of under- and over-tones, while
the guitar gibbered shrilly and hysterically in D natural. Lykeham laughed,
banged down his guitar on to the sofa
with such violence that it gave forth a
trembling groan from all its strings, and
ran forward to meet me. He slapped
me on the shoulder with painful heartiness ; his whole face radiated joy and
excitement.

I can sympathize with people's pains,
but not with their pleasures. There is
something curiously boring about somebody else's happiness.

"You are perspiring," I said coldly.

Lykeham mopped himself, but went
grinning.

" Well, what is it this time ? " I asked. " Are you engaged to be married again ? "

Lykeham burst forth with the triumphant pleasure of one who has at last found an opportunity of disburdening himself of an oppressive secret. " Far better than that," he cried.

I groaned. " Some more than usually unpleasant amour, I suppose." I knew that he had been in London the day before, a pressing engagement with the dentist having furnished an excuse to stay the night.

" Don't be gross," said Lykeham, with a nervous laugh which showed that my suspicions had been only too well founded.

" Well, let's hear about the delectable Flossie or Effie or whatever her name was," I said, with resignation.

" I tell you she was a goddess."

" The goddess of reason, I suppose."

" A goddess," Lykeham continued ; " the most wonderful creature I've ever seen. And the extraordinary thing is," he added confidentially, and with ill-suppressed pride, " that it seems I myself am a god of sorts."

"Of gardens; but do come down to facts."

"I'll tell you the whole story. It was like this : Last night I was in town, you know, and went to see that capital play that's running at the Prince Consort's. It's one of those ingenious combinations of melodrama and problem play, which thrill you to the marrow and at the same time give you a virtuous feeling that you've been to see something serious. Well, I rolled in rather late, having secured an admirable place in the front row of the dress circle. I trampled in over the populace, and casually observed that there was a girl sitting next me, whom I apologized to for treading on her toes. I thought no more about her during the first act. In the interval, when the lights were on again, I turned round to look at things in general and discovered that there was a goddess sitting next me. One only had to look at her to see she was a goddess. She was quite incredibly beautiful—rather pale and virginal and slim, and at the same time very stately. I can't describe her ; she was simply perfect—there's nothing more to be said."

17

" Perfect," I repeated, " but so were all the rest."

" Fool ! " Lykeham answered impatiently. " All the rest were just damned women. This was a goddess, I tell you Don't interrupt me any more. As I was looking with astonishment at her profile, she turned her head and looked squarely at me. I've never seen anything so lovely; I almost swooned away. Our eyes met——"

" What an awful novelist's expression ! " I expostulated.

" I can't help it ; there's no other word. Our eyes did meet, and we both fell simultaneously in love."

" Speak for yourself."

" I could see it in her eyes. Well, to go on. We looked at one another several times during that first interval, and then the second act began. In the course of the act, entirely accidentally, I knocked my programme on to the floor, and reaching down to get it I touched her hand. Well, there was obviously nothing else to do but to take hold of it."

" And what did she do ? "

" Nothing. We sat like that the whole of the rest of the act, rapturously happy and——"

" And quietly perspiring palm to palm. I know exactly, so we can pass over that. Proceed."

" Of course you don't know in the least ; you've never held a goddess's hand. When the lights went up again I reluctantly dropped her hand, not liking the thought of the profane crowd seeing us, and for want of anything better to say, I asked her if she actually was a goddess. She said it was a curious question, as she'd been wondering what god I was. So we said, how incredible : and I said I was sure she was a goddess, and she said she was certain I was a god, and I bought some chocolates, and the third act began. Now, it being a melo-drama, there was of course in the third act a murder and burglary scene, in which all the lights were turned out. In this thrilling moment of total black-ness I suddenly felt her kiss me on the cheek."

" I thought you said she was virginal."

" So she was — absolutely, frozenly

virginal ; but she was made of a sort of burning ice, if you understand me. She was virginally passionate—just the combination you'd expect to find in a goddess. I admit I was startled when she kissed me, but with infinite presence of mind I kissed her back, on the mouth. Then the murder was finished and the lights went on again. Nothing much more happened till the end of the show, when I helped her on with her coat and we went out together, as if it were the most obvious thing in the world, and got into a taxi. I told the man to drive somewhere where we could get supper, and he drove there."

" Not without embracements by the way ? "

" No, not without certain embracements."

" Always passionately virginal ? "

" Always virginally passionate."

" Proceed."

" Well, we had supper—a positively Olympian affair, nectar and ambrosia and stolen hand-pressures. She became more and more wonderful every moment. My God, you should have seen her eyes !

The whole soul seemed to burn in their depths, like fire under the sea——"

"For narrative," I interrupted him, "the epic or heroic style is altogether more suitable than the lyrical."

"Well, as I say, we had supper, and after that my memory becomes a sort of burning mist."

"Let us make haste to draw the inevitable veil. What was her name ? "

Lykeham confessed that he didn't know ; as she was a goddess, it didn't really seem to matter what her earthly name was. How did he expect to find her again ? He hadn't thought of that, but knew she'd turn up somehow. I told him he was a fool, and asked which particular goddess he thought she was and which particular god he himself.

"We discussed that," he said. "We first thought Ares and Aphrodite ; but she wasn't my idea of Aphrodite, and I don't know that I'm very much like Ares."

He looked pensively in the old Venetian mirror which hung over the fireplace. It was a complacent look, for Lykeham was rather vain about his personal appearance, which was, indeed, repulsive at first sight, but had, when you looked again, a certain strange and fascinating ugly beauty. Bearded, he would have made a passable Socrates. But Ares—no, certainly he wasn't Ares.

" Perhaps you're Hephæstus," I suggested ; but the idea was received coldly.

Was he sure that she was a goddess ? Mightn't she just have been a nymph of sorts ? Europa, for instance. Lykeham repudiated the implied suggestion that he was a bull, nor would he hear of himself as a swan or a shower of gold. It was possible, however, he thought, that he was Apollo and she Daphne, reincarnated from her vegetable state. And though I laughed heartily at the idea of his being Phœbus Apollo, Lykeham stuck to the theory with increasing obstinacy. The more he thought of it the more it seemed to him probable that his nymph, with her burning cold virginal passion, was Daphne, while to doubt that he himself was Apollo seemed hardly to occur to him.

It was about a fortnight later, in June,

towards the end of term, that we discovered Lykeham's Olympian identity.
We had gone, Lykeham and I, for an after-dinner walk. We set out through the pale tranquillity of twilight, and following the towpath up the river as far as Godstow, halted at the inn for a glass of port and a talk with the glorious old female Falstaff in black silk who kept it. We were royally entertained with gossip and old wine, and after Lykeham had sung a comic song which had reduced the old lady to a quivering jelly of hysterical laughter, we set out once more, intending to go yet a little farther up the river before we turned back. Darkness had fallen by this time ; the stars were lighted in the sky ; it was the sort of summer night to which Marlowe compared Helen of Troy. Over the meadows invisible peewits wheeled and uttered their melancholy cry ; the far-off thunder of the weir bore a continuous, even burden to all the other small noises of the night. Lykeham and I walked on in silence. We had covered perhaps a quarter of a mile when all at once my companion stopped and began

looking fixedly westward towards
Witham Hill. I paused too, and saw
that he was staring at the thin crescent
of the moon, which was preparing to
set in the dark woods that crowned the
eminence.

"What are you looking at ?" I asked.

But Lykeham paid no attention, only
muttered something to himself. Then
suddenly he cried out, "It's she !" and
started off at full gallop across the fields
in the direction of the hill. Conceiving
that he had gone suddenly mad, I followed. We crashed through the first
hedge twenty yards apart. Then came
the backwater ; Lykeham leapt, flopped
in three-quarters of the way across, and
scrambled oozily ashore. I made a
better jump and landed among the mud
and rushes of the farther bank. Two
more hedges and a ploughed field, a hedge,
a road, a gate, another field, and then we
were in Witham Wood itself. It was
pitch black under the trees, and Lykeham
had perforce to slacken his pace a little.
I followed him by the noise he made
crashing through the undergrowth and
cursing when he hurt himself. That

wood was a nightmare, but we got through it somehow and into the open glade at the top of the hill. Through the trees on the farther side of the clearing shone the moon, seeming incredibly close at hand. Then, suddenly, along the very path of the moonlight, the figure of a woman came walking through the trees into the open. Lykeham rushed towards her and flung himself at her feet and embraced her knees ; she stooped down and smoothed his ruffled hair. I turned and walked away ; it is not for a mere mortal to look on at the embracements of the gods.

As I walked back, I wondered who on earth—or rather who in heaven—Lykeham could be. For here was chaste Cynthia giving herself to him in the most unequivocal fashion. Could he be Endymion ? No, the idea was too preposterous to be entertained for a moment. But I could think of no other loved by the virgin moon. Yet surely I seemed dimly to recollect that there had been some favoured god ; for the life of me I could not remember who. All the way back along the river path I searched my mind for his name, and always it eluded me.

But on my return I looked up the matter in Lemprière, and almost died of laughing when I discovered the truth. I thought of Lykeham's Venetian mirror and his complacent side glances at his own image, and his belief that he was Apollo, and I laughed and laughed. And when, considerably after midnight, Lykeham got back to college, I met him in the porch and took him quietly by the sleeve, and in his ear I whispered, " GOAT-FOOT," and then I roared with laughter once again.

THE BOOKSHOP

IT seemed indeed an unlikely place to find a bookshop. All the other commercial enterprises of the street aimed at purveying the barest necessities to the busy squalor of the quarter. In this, the main arterial street, there was a specious glitter and life produced by the swift passage of the traffic. It was almost airy, almost gay. But all around great tracts of slum pullulated dankly. The inhabitants did their shopping in the grand street; they passed, holding gobbets of meat that showed glutinous even through the wrappings of paper; they cheapened linoleum at upholstery doors; women, black-bonneted and black-shawled, went shuffling to their marketing with dilapidated bags of straw plait. How should these, I wondered, buy books? And yet there it was, a tiny shop; and the windows were fitted with shelves, and there were the brown backs of books.

To the right a large emporium over-
flowed into the street with its fabu-
lously cheap furniture; to the left the
curtained, discreet windows of an eating-
house announced in chipped white
letters the merits of sixpenny dinners.
Between, so narrow as scarcely to prevent
the junction of food and furniture, was
the little shop. A door and four feet of
dark window, that was the full extent
of frontage. One saw here that literature
was a luxury; it took its proportionable
room here in this place of necessity.
Still, the comfort was that it survived,
definitely survived.

The owner of the shop was standing
in the doorway, a little man, grizzle-
bearded and with eyes very active round
the corners of the spectacles that bridged
his long, sharp nose.

" Trade is good ? " I inquired.

" Better in my grandfather's day," he
told me, shaking his head sadly.

" We grow progressively more Philis-
tine," I suggested.

" It is our cheap press. The ephemeral
overwhelms the permanent, the classical."

" This journalism," I agreed, " or call

it rather this piddling quotidianism, is the curse of our age."

" Fit only for——" He gesticulated clutchingly with his hands as though seeking the word.

" For the fire."

The old man was triumphantly emphatic with his, " No : for the sewer."

I laughed sympathetically at his passion. " We are delightfully at one in our views," I told him. " May I look about me a little among your treasures ? "

Within the shop was a brown twilight, redolent with old leather and the smell of that fine subtle dust that clings to the pages of forgotten books, as though preservative of their secrets—like the dry sand of Asian deserts beneath which, still incredibly intact, lie the treasures and the rubbish of a thousand years ago. I opened the first volume that came to my hand. It was a book of fashion-plates, tinted elaborately by hand in magenta and purple, maroon and solferino and puce and those melting shades of green that a yet earlier generation had called " the sorrows of Werther." Beauties in crinolines swam with the amplitude

of pavilioned ships across the pages.
Their feet were represented as thin and
flat and black, like tea-leaves shyly pro-
truding from under their petticoats.
Their faces were egg-shaped, sleeked
round with hair of glossy black, and ex-
pressive of an immaculate purity. I
thought of our modern fashion figures,
with their heels and their arch of instep,
their flattened faces and smile of pouting
invitation. It was difficult not to be a
deteriorationist. I am easily moved by
symbols ; there is something of a Quarles
in my nature. Lacking the philosophic
mind, I prefer to see my abstractions
concretely imaged. And it occurred to
me then that if I wanted an emblem to
picture the sacredness of marriage and
the influence of the home I could not
do better than choose two little black
feet like tea-leaves peeping out decor-
ously from under the hem of wide,
disguising petticoats. While heels and
thoroughbred insteps should figure—oh
well, the reverse.

The current of my thoughts was
turned aside by the old man's voice.
" I expect you are musical," he said.

Oh yes, I was a little; and he held out to me a bulky folio.

"Did you ever hear this?" he asked.

Robert the Devil: no, I never had. I did not doubt that it was a gap in my musical education.

The old man took the book and drew up a chair from the dim *penetralia* of the shop. It was then that I noticed a surprising fact: what I had, at a careless glance, taken to be a common counter I perceived now to be a piano of a square, unfamiliar shape. The old man sat down before it. "You must forgive any defects in its tone," he said, turning to me. "An early Broadwood, Georgian, you know, and has seen a deal of service in a hundred years."

He opened the lid, and the yellow keys grinned at me in the darkness like the teeth of an ancient horse.

The old man rustled pages till he found a desired place. "The ballet music," he said: "it's fine. Listen to this."

His bony, rather tremulous hands began suddenly to move with an astonishing nimbleness, and there rose up, faint and tinkling against the roar of the traffic, a gay pirouetting music. The instrument rattled considerably and the volume of sound was thin as the trickle of a drought-shrunken stream : but, still, it kept tune and the melody was there, filmy, aerial.

"And now for the drinking-song," cried the old man, warming excitedly to his work. He played a series of chords that mounted modulating upwards towards a breaking-point; so supremely operatic as positively to be a parody of that moment of tautening suspense, when the singers are bracing themselves for a burst of passion. And then it came, the drinking chorus. One pictured to oneself cloaked men, wildly jovial over the emptiness of cardboard flagons.

> "Versiam' a tazza piena
> Il generoso umor . . "

The old man's voice was cracked and shrill, but his enthusiasm made up for any defects in execution. I had never seen anyone so wholeheartedly a reveller.

He turned over a few more pages. "Ah, the 'Valse Infernale,'" he said.

" That's good." There was a little melancholy prelude and then the tune, not so infernal perhaps as one might have been led to expect, but still pleasant enough. I looked over his shoulder at the words and sang to his accompaniment.

> " Demoni fatali
> Fantasmi d'orror,
> Dei regni infernali
> Plaudite al signor."

A great steam-driven brewer's lorry roared past with its annihilating thunder and utterly blotted out the last line. The old man's hands still moved over the yellow keys, my mouth opened and shut ; but there was no sound of words or music. It was as though the fatal demons, the phantasms of horror, had made a sudden irruption into this peaceful, abstracted place.

I looked out through the narrow door. The traffic ceaselessly passed ; men and women hurried along with set faces. Phantasms of horror, all of them : infernal realms wherein they dwelt. Outside, men lived under the tyranny of things. Their every action was determined by the orders of mere matter, by money, and the tools of their trade and the unthinking laws of habit and convention. But here I seemed to be safe from things, living at a remove from actuality; here where a bearded old man, improbable survival from some other time, indomitably played the music of romance, despite the fact that the phantasms of horror might occasionally drown the sound of it with their clamour.

"So: will you take it?" The voice of the old man broke across my thoughts. "I will let you have it for five shillings." He was holding out the thick, dilapidated volume towards me. His face wore a look of strained anxiety. I could see how eager he was to get my five shillings, how necessary, poor man! for him. He has been, I thought with an unreasonable bitterness—he has been simply performing for my benefit, like a trained dog. His aloofness, his culture—all a business trick. I felt aggrieved. He was just one of the common phantasms of horror masquerading as the angel of this somewhat comic paradise of contemplation. I gave him a couple of

half-crowns and he began wrapping the
book in paper.

" I tell you," he said, " I'm sorry to
part with it. I get attached to my
books, you know ; but they always have
to go."

He sighed with such an obvious genuine-
ness of feeling that I repented of the
judgment I had passed upon him. He
was a reluctant inhabitant of the infernal
realms, even as was I myself

Outside they were beginning to cry the
evening papers : a ship sunk, trenches
captured, somebody's new stirring
speech. We looked at one another—
the old bookseller and I—in silence. We
understood one another without speech.
Here were we in particular, and here
was the whole of humanity in general,
all faced by the hideous triumph of
things. In this continued massacre of
men, in this old man's enforced sacrifice,
matter equally triumphed. And walking
homeward through Regent's Park, I too
found matter triumphing over me. My
book was unconscionably heavy, and I
wondered what in the world I should do
with a piano score of *Robert the Devil*

when I had got it home. It would only be another thing to weigh me down and hinder me ; and at the moment it was very, oh, abominably, heavy. I leaned over the railings that ring round the ornamental water, and as unostentatiously as I could, I let the book fall into the bushes.

I often think it would be best not to attempt the solution of the problem of life. Living is hard enough without complicating the process by thinking about it. The wisest thing, perhaps, is to take for granted the "wearisome condition of humanity, born under one law, to another bound," and to leave the matter at that, without an attempt to reconcile the incompatibles. Oh, the absurd difficulty of it all! And I have, moreover, wasted five shillings, which is serious, you know, in these thin times.

THE DEATH OF LULLY

T HE sea lay in a breathing calm, and
the galley, bosomed in its transparent water, stirred rhythmically to
the slow pulse of its sleeping life. Down
below there, fathoms away through the
crystal-clear Mediterranean, the shadow
of the ship lazily swung, moving, a long
dark patch, very slowly back and forth
across the white sand of the sea-bottom
—very slowly, a scarcely perceptible
advance and recession of the green darkness. Fishes sometimes passed, now
hanging poised with idly tremulous fins,
now darting onwards, effortless and incredibly swift ; and always, as it seemed,
utterly aimless, whether they rested or
whether they moved ; as the life of
angels their life seemed mysterious and
unknowable.

All was silence on board the ship. In
their fetid cage below decks the rowers
slept where they sat, chained, on their

narrow benches. On deck the sailors
lay sleeping or sat in little groups playing at dice. The fore-part of the deck
was reserved, it seemed, for passengers
of distinction. Two figures, a man and
a woman, were reclining there on couches,
their faces and half-bared limbs flushed
in the coloured shadow that was thrown
by the great red awning stretched above
them.

It was a nobleman, the sailors had
heard, and his mistress that they had
on board. They had taken their passage
at Scanderoon, and were homeward bound
for Spain. Proud as sin these Spaniards
were ; the man treated them like slaves
or dogs. As for the woman, she was
well enough, but they could find as good
a face and pair of breasts in their native
Genoa. If anyone so much as looked at
her from half the ship's length away it
sent her possessor into a rage. He had
struck one man for smiling at her.
Damned Catalonian, as jealous as a stag ;
they wished him the stag's horns as well
as its temper.

It was intensely hot even under the
awning. The man woke from his un-

easy sleep and reached out to where on a little table beside him stood a deep silver cup of mixed wine and water. He drank a gulp of it; it was as warm as blood and hardly cooled his throat. He turned over and, leaning on his elbow, looked at his companion. She on her back, quietly breathing through parted lips, still asleep. He leaned across and pinched her on the breast, so that she woke up with a sudden start and cry of pain.

"Why did you wake me?" she asked.

He laughed and shrugged his shoulders. He had, indeed, had no reason for doing so, except that he did not like it that she should be comfortably asleep, while he was awake and unpleasantly conscious of the heat.

"It is hotter than ever," he said, with a kind of gloomy satisfaction at the thought that she would now have to suffer the same discomforts as himself. "The wine scorches instead of cooling; the sun seems no lower down the sky."

The woman pouted. "You pinched me cruelly," she said. "And I still do not know why you wanted to wake me."

He smiled again, this time with a good-humoured lasciviousness. "I wanted to kiss you," he said. He passed his hand over her body possessively, as a man might caress a dog.

Suddenly the quiet of the afternoon was shattered. A great clamour rose up, ragged and uneven, on the air. Shrill yells pierced the dull rumbling growl of bass voices, pierced the sound of beaten drums and hammered metal.

"What are they doing in the town?" asked the woman anxiously of her lover.

"God knows," he answered. "Perhaps the heathen hounds are making some trouble with our men."

He got up and walked to the rail of the ship. A quarter of a mile away, across the smooth water of the bay, stood the little African town at which they had stopped to call. The sunlight showed everything with a hard and merciless definition. Sky, palms, white houses, domes, and towers seemed as though made from some hard enamelled metal. A ridge of low red hills rolled away to right and left. The sunshine gave to everything in the scene the same clarity of detail, so that to the eye of the onlooker there was no impression of distance. The whole thing seemed to be painted in flat upon a single plane.

The young man returned to his couch under the awning and lay down. It was hotter than ever, or seemed so, at least, since he had made the exertion of getting up. He thought of high cool pastures in the hills, with the pleasant sound of streams, far down and out of sight in their deep channels. He thought of winds that were fresh and scented— winds that were not mere breaths of dust and fire. He thought of the shade of cypresses, a narrow opaque strip of darkness ; and he thought too of the green coolness, more diffused and fluid and transparent, of chestnut groves. And he thought of the people he remembered sitting under the trees—young people, gay and brightly dressed, whose life was all gaiety and deliciousness. There were the songs that they sang—he recalled the voices and the dancing of the strings. And there were perfumes and, when one drew closer, the faint intoxicating fragrance of a woman's body. He thought of

the stories they told ; one in particular
came to his mind, a capital tale of a
sorcerer who offered to change a peasant's
wife into a mare, and how he gulled the
husband and enjoyed the woman before his
eyes, and the delightful excuses he made
when she failed to change her shape. He
smiled to himself at the thought of it, and
stretching out a hand touched his mistress.
Her bosom was soft to his fingers and damp
with sweat ; he had an unpleasant notion
that she was melting in the heat.

" Why do you touch me ? " she asked.

He made no reply, but turned away
from her. He wondered how it would
come to pass that people would rise again
in the body. It seemed curious, consider-
ing the manifest activities of worms. And
suppose one rose in the body that one
possessed in age. He shuddered, pictur-
ing to himself what this woman would be
like when she was sixty, seventy. She
would be beyond words repulsive. Old
men too were horrible. They stank, and
their eyes were rheumy and rosiny, like
the eyes of deer. He decided that he
would kill himself before he grew old.
He was eight-and-twenty now. He would

give himself twelve years more. Then he would end it. His thoughts dimmed and faded away into sleep.

The woman looked at him as he slept. He was a good man, she thought, though sometimes cruel. He was different from all the other men she had known. Once, when she was sixteen and a beginner in the business of love, she had thought that all men were always drunk when they made love. They were all dirty and like beasts; she had felt herself superior to them. But this man was a nobleman. She could not understand him; his thoughts were always obscure. She felt herself infinitely inferior to him. She was afraid of him and his occasional cruelty; but still he was a good man, and he might do what he liked with her.

From far off came the sound of oars, a rhythmical splash and creak. Somebody shouted, and from startlingly close at hand one of the sailors hallooed back.

The young man woke up with a start.

"What is it?" he asked, turning with an angry look to the girl, as though he held her to be responsible for this breaking in upon his slumbers.

" The boat, I think," she said. " It must be coming back from the shore."

The boat's crew came up over the side, and all the stagnant life of the ship flowed excitedly round them. They were the centre of a vortex towards which all were drawn. Even the young Catalonian, for all his hatred of these stinking Genoese shipmen, was sucked into the eddy. Everybody was talking at once, and in the general hubbub of question and answer there was nothing coherent to be made out. Piercingly distinct above all the noise came the voice of the little cabin-boy, who had been to shore with the boat's crew. He was running round to everyone in turn repeating: " I hit one of them. You know. I hit one. With a stone on the forehead. Didn't he bleed, ooh! didn't he just ! " And he would dance with uncontrollable excitement.

The captain held up his hand and shouted for silence. " One at a time, there," he ordered, and when order had a little been restored, added grumblingly, " Like a pack of dogs on a bone. You talk, boatswain."

" I hit one of them," said the boy.

Somebody cuffed him over the head,
and he relapsed into silence.

When the boatswain's story had
rambled through labyrinths of digression,
over countless obstacles of interruptions
and emendations, to its conclusion, the
Spaniard went back to join his companion
under the awning. He had assumed
again his habitual indifference.

"Nearly butchered," he said languidly,
in response to her eager questions.
"They"—he jerked a hand in the
direction of the town—"they were
pelting an old fellow who had come there
preaching the Faith. Left him dead
on the beach. Our men had to run
for it."

She could get no more out of him; he
turned over and pretended to go to sleep.

Towards evening they received a visit
from the captain. He was a large, handsome man, with gold ear-rings glinting
from among a bush of black hair.

"Divine Providence," he remarked
sententiously, after the usual courtesies
had passed, "has called upon us to perform a very notable work."

" Indeed ? " said the young man.

" No less a work," continued the captain, " than to save from the clutches of the infidels and heathen the precious remains of a holy martyr."

The captain let fall his pompous manner. It was evident that he had carefully prepared these pious sentences, they rolled so roundly off his tongue. But he was eager now to get on with his story, and it was in a homelier style that he went on : " If you knew these seas as well as I—and it's near twenty years now that I've been sailing them —you'd have some knowledge of this same holy man that — God rot their souls for it !—these cursed Arabs have done to death here. I've heard of him more than once in my time, and not always well spoken of ; for, to tell the honest truth, he does more harm with his preachments to good Christian traders than ever he did good to black-hearted heathen dogs. Leave the bees alone, I say, and if you can get a little honey out of them quietly, so much the better ; but he goes about among the beehives with a pole, stirring up trouble for him-

self and others too. Leave them alone
to their damnation, is what I say, and
get what you can from them this side of
hell. But, still, he has died a holy
martyr's death. God rest his soul! A
martyr is a wonderful thing, you know,
and it's not for the likes of us to understand what they mean by it all.

" They do say, too, that he could make
gold. And, to my mind, it would have
been a thing more pleasing to God and
man if he had stopped at home minting
money for poor folks and dealing it
round, so that there'd be no need to
work any more and break oneself for a
morsel of bread. Yes, he was great at
gold-making and at the books too. They
tell me he was called the Illuminated
Doctor. But I know him still as plain
Lully. I used to hear of him from my
father, plain Lully, and no better once
than he should have been.

" My father was a shipwright in
Minorca in those days—how long since ?
Fifty, sixty years perhaps. He knew him
then ; he has often told me the tale. And
a raffish young dog he was. Drinking,
drabbing, and dicing he outdid them

all, and between the bouts wrote poems,
they say, which was more than the rest
could do. But he gave it all up on the
sudden. Gave away his lands, quitted his
former companions, and turned hermit
up in the hills, living alone like a fox in
his burrow, high up above the vines.
And all because of a woman and his
own qualmish stomach."

The shipmaster paused and helped
himself to a little wine. "And what
did this woman do ? " the girl asked
curiously.

"Ah, it's not what she did but what
she didn't do," the captain answered,
with a leer and wink. "She kept him
at his distance—all but once, all but
once ; and that was what put him on
the road to being a martyr. But there,
I'm outrunning myself. I must go more
soberly.

"There was a lady of some consequence
in the island—one of the Castellos, I
think she was ; her first name has quite
slipped my memory—Anastasia, or something of the kind. Lully conceives a
passion for her, and sighs and importunes
her through I know not how many

months and years.   But her virtue stands
steady as the judgment seat.   Well, in
the end, what happens was this.   The
story leaked out after it was all over, and
he was turned hermit in the mountains.
What happened, I say, was this.   She
tells him at last that he may come and
see her, fixing some solitary twilight
place and time, her own room at night-
fall.   You can guess how he washes and
curls and scents himself, shaves his chin,
chews anises, musks over whatever of
the goat may cling about the body.   Off
he goes, dreaming swoons and ecstasies,
foretasting inconceivable sweets.   Arrived,
he finds the lady a little melancholy—
her settled humour, but a man might
expect a smile at such a time.   Still,
nothing abashed, he falls at her feet and
pours out his piteous case, telling her he
has sighed through seven years, not closed
an eye for above a hundred nights, is
forepined to a shadow, and, in a word,
will perish unless she show some mercy.
She, still melancholy — her settled
humour, mark you—makes answer that
she is ready to yield, and that her body is
entirely his.   With that, she lets herself

be done with as he pleases, but always sorrowfully. 'You are all mine,' says he — 'all mine '—and unlaces her gorgeret to prove the same. But he was wrong. Another lover was already in her bosom, and his kisses had been passionate—oh, burning passionate, for he had kissed away half her left breast. From the nipple down it had all been gnawed away by a cancer.

" Bah, a man may see as bad as that any day in the street or at church-doors where beggars most congregate. I grant you that it is a nasty sight, worm-eaten flesh, but still — not enough, you will agree, to make yourself a hermit over. But there, I told you he had a queasiness of the stomach. But doubtless it was all in God's plan to make a holy martyr of him. But for that same queasiness of his, he would still be living there, a superannuated rake; or else have died in very foul odour, instead of passing, all embalmed with sanctity, to Paradise Gate.

" I know not what happened to him between his hermit-hood and his quest for martyrdom. I saw him first a dozen

years ago, down Tunis way. They were
always clapping him into prison or pulling
out his beard for preaching. This time,
it seems, they have made a holy martyr
of him, done the business thoroughly
with no bungling. Well, may he pray
for our souls at the throne of God. I
go in secretly to-night to steal his body.
It lies on the shore there beyond the
jetty. It will be a notable work, I tell
you, to bring back so precious a corpse
to Christendom. A most notable
work. . . ."

The captain rubbed his hands.

It was after midnight, but there was
still a bustle of activity on board the
galley. At any moment they were ex-
pecting the arrival of the boat with the
corpse of the martyr. A couch, neatly
draped in black, with at its head and foot
candles burning two by two, had been set
out on the poop for the reception of the
body. The captain called the young
Spaniard and his mistress to come and
see the bier.

"That's a good bit of work for you,"
he said, with justifiable pride. "I defy

anyone to make a more decent resting-place for a martyr than that is. It could hardly have been done better on shore, with every appliance at hand. But we sailors, you know, can make anything out of nothing. A truckle-bed, a strip of tarred canvas, and four tallow dips from the cabin lanterns—there you are, a bier for a king."

He hurried away, and a little later the young man and the girl could hear him giving orders and cursing some-where down below. The candles burned almost without a tremor in the windless air, and the reflections of the stars were long, thin tracks of fire along the utterly calm water.

"Were there but perfumed flowers and the sound of a lute," said the young Spaniard, " the night would tremble into passion of its own accord. Love should come unsought on such a night as this, among these black waters and the stars that sleep so peacefully on their bosom."

He put his arm round the girl and bent his head to kiss her. But she averted her face. He could feel a shudder run her through the body.

" Not to-night," she whispered. " I
think of the poor dead man. I would
rather pray."

" No, no," he cried. " Forget him.
Remember only that we are alive, and
that we have but little time and none
to waste."

He drew her into the shadow under
the bulwark, and, sitting down on a coil
of rope, crushed her body to his own and
began kissing her with fury. She lay,
at first, limp in his arms, but gradually she
kindled to his passion.

A plash of oars announced the approach
of the boat. The captain hallooed into
the darkness : " Did you find him ? "

" Yes, we have him here," came back
the answer.

" Good. Bring him alongside and
we'll hoist him up. We have the bier in
readiness. He shall lie in state to-night."

" But he's not dead," shouted back
the voice from the night.

" Not dead ? " repeated the captain,
thunderstruck. " But what about the
bier, then ? "

A thin, feeble voice came back.
" **Your work will not be wasted, my friend**

It will be but a short time before I need your bier."

The captain, a little abashed, answered in a gentler tone, " We thought, holy father, that the heathens had done their worst and that Almighty God had already given you the martyr's crown."

By this time the boat had emerged from the darkness. In the stern sheets an old man was lying, his white hair and beard stained with blood, his Dominican's robe torn and fouled with dust. At the sight of him, the captain pulled off his cap and dropped upon his knees.

" Give us your blessing, holy father," he begged.

The old man raised his hand and wished him peace.

They lifted him on board and, at his own desire, laid him upon the bier which had been prepared for his dead body. " It would be a waste of trouble," he said, " to put me anywhere else, seeing I shall in any case be lying there so soon."

So there he lay, very still under the four candles. One might have taken him for dead already, but that his eyes, when he opened them, shone so brightly.

He dismissed from the poop everyone except the young Spaniard. "We
are countrymen," he said, "and of
noble blood, both of us. I would
rather have you near me than anyone
else."

The sailors knelt for a blessing and
disappeared; soon they could be heard
weighing the anchor; it was safest to be
off before day. Like mourners at either
side of the lighted bier crouched the
Spaniard and his mistress. The body of
the old man, who was not yet dead, lay
quiet under the candles. The martyr was
silent for some time, but at last he opened
his eyes and looked at the young man
and the woman.

"I too," he said, "was in love, once.
In this year falls the jubilee of my last
earthly passion; fifty years have run since
last I longed after the flesh—fifty years
since God opened my eyes to the hideous-
ness of the corruption that man has
brought upon himself.

"You are young, and your bodies are
clean and straight, with no blotch or ulcer
or leprous taint to mar their much-desired
beauty; but because of your outward

pride, your souls, it may be, fester inwardly the more.

"And yet God made all perfect ; it is but accident and the evil of will that causes defaults. All metals should be gold, were it not that their elements willed evilly in their desire to combine. And so with men : the burning sulphur of passion, the salt of wisdom, the nimble mercurial soul should come together to make a golden being, incorruptible and rustless. But the elements mingle jarringly, not in a pure harmony of love, and gold is rare, while lead and iron and poisonous brass that leaves a taste as of remorse behind it are everywhere common.

"God opened my eyes to it before my youth had too utterly wasted itself to rottenness. It was half a hundred years ago, but I see her still, my Ambrosia, with her white, sad face and her naked body and that monstrous ill eating away at her breast.

"I have lived since then trying to amend the evil, trying to restore, as far as my poor powers would go, some measure of original perfection to the corrupted world. I have striven to give to all metals their true

nature, to make true gold from the false,
the unreal, the accidental metals, lead and
copper and tin and iron. And I have
essayed that more difficult alchemy, the
transformation of men. I die now in
my effort to purge away that most foul
dross of misbelief from the souls of these
heathen men. Have I achieved anything?
I know not."

The galley was moving now, its head
turned seaward. The candles shivered in
the wind of its speed, casting uncertain,
changing shadows upon his face. There
was a long silence on the poop. The oars
creaked and splashed. Sometimes a
shout would come up from below, orders
given by the overseer of the slaves, a curse,
the sound of a blow. The old man spoke
again, more weakly now, as though to
himself.

" I have had eighty years of it," he said—
" eighty years in the midst of this cor-
roding sea of hatred and strife. A man
has need to keep pure and unalloyed his
core of gold, that little centre of perfection with which all, even in this de-
clination of time, are born. All other
metal, though it be as tough as steel,

as shining-hard as brass, will melt before the devouring bitterness of life. Hatred, lust, anger—the vile passions will corrode your will of iron, the warlike pomp of your front of brass. It needs the golden perfection of pure love and pure knowledge to withstand them.

" God has willed that I should be the stone—weak, indeed, in virtue—that has touched and transformed at least a little of baser metal into the gold that is above corruption. But it is hard work—thankless work. Man has made a hell of his world, and has set up gods of pain to rule it. Goatish gods, that revel and feast on the agony of it all, poring over the tortured world, like those hateful lovers, whose lust burns darkly into cruelty.

" Fever goads us through life in a delirium of madness. Thirsting for the swamps of evil whence the fever came, thirsting for the mirages of his own delirium, man rushes headlong he knows not whither. And all the time a devouring cancer gnaws at his entrails. It will kill him in the end, when even the ghastly inspiration of fever will not be enough to whip him on. He will lie there, cumbering the earth, a heap of rottenness and pain, until at last the cleansing fire comes to sweep the horror away.

" Fever and cancer ; acids that burn and corrode. . . . I have had eighty years of it. Thank God, it is the end."

It was already dawn ; the candles were hardly visible now in the light, faded to nothing, like souls in prosperity. In a little while the old man was asleep.

The captain tiptoed up on to the poop and drew the young Spaniard aside for a confidential talk.

" Do you think he will die to-day ? " he asked.

The young man nodded.

" God rest his soul," said the captain piously. " But do you think it would be best to take his body to Minorca or to Genoa ? At Minorca they would give much to have their own patron martyr. At the same time it would add to the glory of Genoa to possess so holy a relic, though he is in no way connected with the place. It's there is my difficulty. Suppose, you see, that my people of Genoa did not want the body, he being from Minorca and not one of them. I should

look a fool then, bringing it in in state.
Oh, it's hard, it's hard. There's so much
to think about. I am not sure but
what I hadn't better put in at Minorca
first. What do you think ? "

The Spaniard shrugged his shoulders.
" I have no advice to offer."

" Lord," said the captain as he bustled
away, " life is a tangled knot to unravel."